The Astral Fortress

Mitch Booker

6-18-83

TOM SWIFT®
THE ASTRAL FORTRESS
VICTOR APPLETON

WANDERER BOOKS
Published by Simon & Schuster, New York

Published by WANDERER BOOKS
A Simon & Schuster Division of
Gulf & Western Corporation
Simon & Schuster Building
1230 Avenue of the Americas
New York, New York 10020

Manufactured in the United States of America
10 9 8 7 6 5 4 3 2 1

WANDERER and colophon are trademarks of Simon & Schuster

TOM SWIFT is a trademark of Stratemeyer Syndicate, registered in
the United States Patent and Trademark Office

Library of Congress Cataloging in Publication Data
Appleton, Victor, pseud.
The astral fortress.

(Tom Swift ; no. 5)
Summary: When Tom Swift and his crew jump back from
the Alpha Centauri system through hyperspace to the
Earth's galaxy, they are captured by their arch enemy
David Luna and taken prisoner aboard his astral fortress.
[1. Science fiction] I. Title. II. Series: Appleton,
Victor, pseud. Tom Swift ; no. 5.
PZ7.A652As   [Fic]   81–16645
ISBN 0–671–43369–5   AACR2
ISBN 0–671–43385–7 (pbk.)

CONTENTS

Chapter One

"You realize no human being has ever done what we are about to do?" The speaker, Tom Swift, turned from the control panel of his starship, the *Exedra,* and faced his friends.

The crew looked at him tensely. Each knew they were facing unknown dangers, yet they all had faith in the young inventor.

"I know we used the stardrive to jump through hyperspace from Earth's galaxy to the Alpha Centauri system where we are now," Tom explained. "But returning to Earth might be different."

"I don't see how it would be different," said Kate Reiko One Star. The tall, beautiful Indian girl with the almond-shaped eyes inherited from her Japanese mother shifted in her seat. "Of course, I'm not a scientist like the rest of you, but isn't a jump through the walls of space just a jump through the walls of space?"

"Not exactly," her cousin, Benjamin Franklin Walking Eagle, put in. "You see, we tested the stardrive to take off from the conditions in our own solar system. The solar system of the Skree is different. What worked in one place might not work in another."

"On the other hand, we have the expert advice of the people who first built the stardrive, the Skree themselves," Tom added.

Everyone looked at the being who would be the first alien to set foot on planet Earth—that is, if the jump through hyperspace worked. Mok N'Ghai, commander in the Skree military and personal friend of the Royal Family, looked like a seven-foot-long insect, but everyone on board had come to admire his intelligence and graciousness. Fighting with the Skree forces against the Chutans, their enemies (told in *Tom Swift: The War in Outer Space*), had convinced the young people that outward appearances were really not important.

The alien shifted in his contour couch and merely nodded.

"Tom, the final calculations have been triple checked. All systems are go." Aristotle, Tom's robot and favorite invention (built and tested in the midst of great danger in *Tom Swift: Terror on the Moons of Jupiter*) swiveled his head around completely. His camera eyes flashed in Tom's face. "Though I do not technically have a vote in this matter, I should like to say at this time I concur with the general sentiment. I am anxious to once again return to the place of my birth—er, my creation."

Everyone laughed and Ben put his hands on the computer terminal, which he knew as well as he knew his own Indian heritage. "We've done all the advance work we could," he urged. "We'll never be more ready than we are right now."

Tom turned to the one member of the crew who had not yet spoken. "Anita, do you agree?" he asked.

The beautiful redhead's eyes twinkled with excitement. "Of course. What are we waiting for?"

"Okay, Ben," Tom said to his copilot. "Begin countdown to stardrive engagement."

The young computer technician depressed a small, black lever. Everyone settled back into the padded contour couches, holding their breath.

"Thirty seconds to hyperspace jump," came

the mechanical voice of the automatic warning system. "Twenty-nine, twenty-eight, twenty-seven . . ."

Tom smiled at Ben and gave him the thumbs-up sign.

Ben returned the smile but could not keep a line of nervous perspiration from forming above his upper lip.

"Fifteen seconds, fourteen, thirteen, twelve . . ." the voice droned on.

A thousand disconnected thoughts flew through Tom Swift's mind. As captain of the *Exedra,* he was responsible not only for the starship but also for the lives of his friends. What if their calculations were off? Even the tiniest error might mean they would miss the Earth's galaxy. It might very well mean they would all end up in some part of space so far from Earth they would be unable even to plot a course to return home. They would be lost—hopelessly—forever; out of communication with family and friends.

Stop it! he told himself sternly. Concentrate! Get ready for the crushing gravity forces that will try and squeeze all the breath from your body.

"Five seconds, four, three, two, one. Engage stardrive."

Suddenly, Tom felt a maddening, unbearable pressure grow behind his tightly closed eyes. He forced himself to open them and watch the readouts on the *Exedra*'s control panel. It was useless to study the rapidly changing indicators. The starship's instruments had gone crazy the moment it entered hyperspace.

The young inventor counted the passing seconds to himself and fought to keep from losing consciousness. Jumping through hyperspace was almost like existing inside a photographic negative. Everything was the opposite from the worlds he knew. Black was white, up was down, and everything swirled and jumped so rapidly it was impossible to get his bearings. Everything was inside out.

Tom's body ached, his ears rang. He fought hard not to get sick.

Just when he began to black out—it was quite suddenly all over. The pain and discomfort were gone. His surroundings became familiar again.

"We're home!" shouted Ben. He began to tap the keys of his computer terminal quickly. "I'll check to find out exactly where we are."

"Whew! I don't think I'll *ever* get used to that trick!" exclaimed Kate.

"Me, neither," Anita agreed, shaking her long red hair. "But I'm sure glad we can do it!"

Tom scanned the printout on the screen in front of him. "We're still outside the asteroid belt." He laughed. "I'd say we're not quite home yet!"

"The navigation instruments have locked onto the good ol' Sun, though," Ben said. "If everything stays normal, we'll be home before you know it!"

"Did I hear you say *the* Sun?" asked Anita. "Shouldn't we get into the habit of calling it *our* sun or Sol? 'The Sun' makes it sound like the only sun in space. Now that we've just returned from another galaxy where there are other suns and where planets with intelligent beings circle those suns, we ought to become more sophisticated about calling things by their proper names."

The beautiful redhead unbuckled her restraining harness and stretched. The *Exedra* was too small to have artificial gravity, so her movement propelled the young woman out of her padded couch. Since Anita was an expert in maneuvering in free-fall, she preferred not to use weighted or magnetic boots inside the ship. Instead, she tucked her body into a tight ball to gain directional control, and then straightened up, grabbing a nearby handhold on the bulkhead as she sailed by.

Ben looked at her and grinned mischievously. "You can become as sophisticated as you want to! As for me, I'm just a small-town guy. I can hardly wait to see my family and sit down to some of my mom's fried squash blossoms." He looked at Mok N'Ghai and blushed. "That's not to say the food on your home planet of Kosanth was bad or anything," he added hastily to the alien.

Tom glanced at the Skree warrior, still not quite believing that he not only knew, but could converse with, a true alien. A real, nonmovie, not-a-man-in-a-funny-rubber-suit alien. The fact that the intelligent Skree looked something like a seven-foot praying mantis was something they had all finally become used to.

Well, almost.

Maybe no human being could ever really become accustomed to a tall insectile that was highly intelligent and very charming. Any xenophobia—fear of strangers—that Tom might have had upon first meeting the Skree had dissipated after their adventures with Mok N'Ghai.

"I quite understand your feeling, Ben," the Skree commander said. He worked his mandibles in his favorite expression of amusement. "I was once marooned for several hours on a tiny, out-of-the-way planet because my shuttle ship developed a mechanical problem. The only food available at the time happened to be the great gourmet delicacy of the planet. The natives called it 'lapchis,' I think. To me, unfortunately, it tasted like clay mixed with heavy lubricating oil. It was quite safe, though, and I had to eat a bit of it to be diplomatic. But I was very happy to get back to my ship!"

Everyone laughed and Mok N'Ghai continued his story. "I immediately ordered up a huge platter of my favorite vegetables and ate as though I had been starved for days."

The alien was wearing a specially adapted TTU—Teacher-Translator Unit—that translated from English into Skree. Tom had invented the device to solve the language problems he knew he and his friends would be faced with once they began contacting alien civilizations in their space travels. They had worn the TTUs while communicating with the Skree and the devices had functioned perfectly.

The exceptional thing about the invention was its dual purpose. On the translating mode, it interpreted whatever was being spoken into the language of the wearer. But it also contained a learning mode, which could teach the wearer the unfamiliar tongue quickly.

Mok N'Ghai knew some English, although it was heavily accented. The alien spoke it slowly in order to have the proper pronunciation, but Tom had to admire the progress he had made.

The structure of the Skree's face and jaws was designed for a language quite different from anything spoken on Earth.

For his part, Tom was struggling valiantly with Skree. He could talk in simple sentences and he was working hard to increase his vocabulary. It was not as difficult to learn as English. But Tom had a problem similar to Mok N'Ghai's. "It's like trying to speak while drinking water and imitating a grumpy pigeon," he once told Ben.

Tom's attention was now drawn to Mok N'Ghai's fumbling with the catch on his restraining harness. It was made for human hands, which were more flexible, but weaker, than the formidable Skree fingers.

Kate One Star reached over and deftly flipped the catch. It made Tom think for a moment. "You know," he mused aloud, "if visitors from other planets start coming to Earth regularly, a lot of everyday items will have to be redesigned or adapted for their use."

"You mean like the United States did back in the twentieth century when they began installing ramps and lowering telephones for people in wheelchairs?" Anita put in.

"Looks like Swift Enterprises will have its hands full anticipating all those technical changes," Ben added.

"And we'll have to become more tolerant and adaptive if we want to go visit their worlds," Tom added.

"I think the proper term is pangalactic," Aristotle said.

As Tom quickly scanned the controls in front of him, he thought about the future. Mankind was just one of the many different intelligent life forms in the galaxy. Some were probably more intelligent, some perhaps less. But they would all be "people," no matter how odd their exteriors might appear to people from Earth. Intelligence was a common bond across species, across space. Mok N'Ghai and the other friends they had made among the Skree were proof of that.

Aristotle suddenly rotated his mainframe and spoke to Tom. "Excuse me, but I have picked up some very disturbing blips on my navigation screen. I think you should take a look immediately."

"Asteroids?" Tom asked the logical question.

"No. They are moving much too fast and too . . ." The mechanoid paused to select the exact word. "Too deliberately in our direction."

"Deliberately?" Ben asked.

"Yes," the robot said without hesitation. "Unlike myself, the *Exedra*'s main computer does not make errors."

Tom raised his eyebrows but said nothing. Aristotle's inferiority complex was rooted somewhere deep in his complex circuitry. The young inventor had spent many hours unsuccessfully trying to ferret out that bug in his beloved invention.

"Put them on the main screen, maximum solar filter," he commanded.

The excited chatter on the bridge died as all eyes and sensors concentrated on the ten blips that were suddenly moving across the screen.

"Those are spaceships in fighting formation!" Kate One Star shouted.

"And they are headed straight at us, approaching at almost unbelievable speeds!" Ben said grimly.

Chapter Two

"Are you sure?" Tom asked. "Double-check all incoming information on the objects in question."

"Information is confirmed," Aristotle said.

"That is a fighting formation if ever I've seen one," insisted Kate. "And believe me, I've seen a lot of fighting formations in my time." She pushed her long, straight, black hair over her right shoulder and twisted it around her fingers —a sure sign she was thinking hard.

Tom knew that, as a combat specialist, Ben's cousin was an expert on survival under hostile conditions and had considerably more experience dealing with this kind of situation than any of them. He searched her handsome face for signs of worry, but found none. Her expression was one of watchfulness.

But if she was right, they had a lot to worry about!

"We can't be in this much trouble just for leaving Alpha Centauri without permission!" Ben protested. He keyed a request for the identity of the approaching vessels into the computer.

Tom watched Ben's message appear on the monitor and held his breath.

The computer's reply was speedy: NEGATIVE DATA AVAILABLE.

"I half expected that," Tom said quietly.

Ben turned to him, openmouthed in surprise.

"Try again, Ben. Just to make sure there was no, shall we say, misunderstanding, between man and machine."

Ben thought for a second, then his fingers once again flew over the keyboard, rephrasing his request.

NEGATIVE DATA AVAILABLE, came the answer once again.

"Ask it why," Tom said quickly.

Ben keyed the request.

SHIP-TO-SHIP TRANSMISSION CAPABILITY TEMPORARILY TERMINATED.

REASON FOR TERMINATION Ben typed, without waiting to be asked.

NEGATIVE DATA AVAILABLE blinked the screen.

Ben sat back in his couch and stared out into the blackness of space through the reinforced glassite port.

Tom knew his best friend was stumped. That almost never happened to Benjamin Franklin Walking Eagle. To other computer techs, yes, but not to Ben. Ben could explore even the most private circuits of any computer with one hand tied behind his back. Their secrets were never safe from him.

"They'll be close enough for visual identification soon," Tom said. "Let's see if they'll answer our call."

The young man opened the *Exedra*'s audio channels. "*Exedra* to approaching vessels, *Exedra* to approaching vessels: identify yourselves. Over," he said.

Nothing but the unbroken static of space came over the open channel.

"Commander."

Tom turned, surprised to see Mok N'Ghai floating weightlessly beside him. The flashing lights from the control panel were being reflected off the alien's large, multifaceted eyes. The bright blue, red, orange, and green indicators were the only lights on in the bridge at that moment, and the effect made the Skree ambassador look like something out of a horror movie.

"It is difficult to interpret the actions of the approaching fleet as anything but hostile," the alien said. "Your restraint is most admirable."

Tom shook his head somewhat ruefully. "The *Exedra* is not exactly a battle cruiser like your *Sword of Death*," Tom said, momentarily recalling his first meeting with the Skree commander outside the Alpha Centauri system. "This is just a small, fighter-class vessel. Our options are very limited."

"I have more data on the approaching vessels, Tom," Aristotle broke in. "There are nine fighter-class ships and one larger vessel at the apex of the formation. It seems to be the center of communication."

"The flagship," Tom commented. "Can you pick up their communications?"

"Yes. However, they are in code. I am in the process of deciphering them," the robot added.

Tom stared uneasily at the mysterious fleet of approaching ships. He felt a peculiar sensation, a tingling at the back of his neck that occasionally turned into a chill running down his spine. A warning of his sixth sense, he supposed, while his other five senses were working overtime.

The distances in space were so vast that nothing was going to happen immediately. Tom could not yet even see the visual details of the ships.

"Go to full magnification on the large ship," he told Aristotle. "The resolution won't be very good, but—" The young inventor stopped in midsentence as a chilling image appeared on the screen.

"What is it?" Anita asked, alarm creeping into her voice. "It looks like a ship, but it has a huge landing platform, like an old-time Navy carrier!"

"It's some kind of a space fortress!" Tom exclaimed in wonderment. "But I can't make out any identification or markings anywhere on it. Wait!" He gasped suddenly. "There's something . . ." His voice trailed off as he peered at the mysterious vessel intently.

The high magnification was distorting small details and Tom strained to see what looked like an emblem painted on the broad, flat surface of the landing platform.

"It's not a Navy vessel," the young inventor said, not taking his eyes from the screen. The seconds seemed to crawl by like hours as the giant ship grew larger on the screen. "As far as I know, the Navy does not have anything like this in construction."

Kate gasped, interrupting his thought. "I don't believe it!" she exclaimed.

Tom's eyes widened as he noticed the white

circle pierced by a sword on a field of speckled black. It was the emblem of his arch enemy, the evil millionaire industrialist, David Luna!

Before their trip to Alpha Centauri, Kate had almost been tricked into working for the villain, but when she learned the truth about him, she had joined Tom and his friends. Their adventure had begun so suddenly, she had not even had time to change her clothes. She still wore the uniform of Luna's private guard, a white jump-suit with his corporation emblem on its epaulets.

"I thought Luna had disappeared mysteriously from Earth," Anita spoke up.

"Yes, and now he's evidently hiding out in the asteroid belt," Ben said.

Tom did not need to look at the gun-metal gray apparition on the screen any longer. "I have a hunch we'll be getting answers to all of our questions very soon. Battle stations!" he commanded.

His friends reacted instantly. Ben left Aristotle in charge of the main computer and moved to the forward laser turret where he strapped himself in firmly. The young Indian immediately began readying the cannon.

Anita and Kate launched themselves aft. Tom heard them relay their readiness from the ship's rear cannons over the communications system.

"I'm all set," Anita said. That meant she had plugged her personal computer into the battle computer terminal of her laser cannon. Anita had been the unfortunate victim of a childhood accident and her right leg was amputated below the knee. Through the miracle of technology, an artificial leg, powered by a computer, enabled her to lead a normal, active life.

The basic function of the computer was to translate signals from Anita's nervous system into electrical impulses for normal movement in the artificial limb. But Anita had chosen to expand the capabilities of the computer. She was now linked up to her laser cannon and it was tied directly into her own nervous system through the computer. She and the laser cannon were almost one. It was an extension of her body.

"I feel useless!" said Mok N'Ghai. "I may have been sent to your world as a peace ambassador, but, by profession, I am a soldier and the commander of a starship. I do not wish to be a mere spectator in this battle, Tom. Please assign me to a duty station!"

Tom indicated the vacant copilot's couch next to him. "I could use your help," he said. "We are badly outnumbered and I need the benefit of your experience."

The alien nodded in silent acknowledgement

and settled himself into Ben's place. Tom helped him strap in. Together, they examined the computer monitor where the battle computer displayed the formation of the approaching ships.

"They seek to encircle us, I think," Mok N'Ghai pointed out. The alien traced the outline of the formation with his finger. It was now a "C" shape, and the open ends were moving closer and closer together like giant pincers. On its present course, the *Exedra* was headed straight for that fatal gap!

Chapter Three

"All hands stand by for evasive maneuvers!" shouted Tom as he pulled down hard on the *Exedra*'s planetary drive control. The sleek starship leaped forward like something alive, pinning her passengers against their acceleration couches.

On the computer screen, the dot of light that represented the *Exedra* remained in the center of the screen, while the approaching ships suddenly disappeared from it. The screen was momentarily blank as the computer adjusted its display for the distance Tom had put between his ship and the pursuing fleet.

Tom eased off the control and breathed deeply, partly from relief, but mostly because the tremendous g-force had made it very difficult to breathe.

His relief was short-lived. A sudden crackling of static came from the ship's radio. Then a voice, which Tom recognized as that of David Luna, chuckled.

"You got away from me outside *New America* because the *Exedra* is truly a remarkable ship, Tom. But I haven't been idle while you were away!" Luna announced.

Mok N'Ghai made a sound of dismay and pointed to the computer screen. Tom felt a tightening in his stomach. As he watched, the fleet of ships began rapidly closing in on the *Exedra*.

Tom hit the controls and the ship surged powerfully ahead.

"You can't keep running away from me forever," Luna chided.

"I'd know that slimy voice anywhere," Tom heard Anita snarl.

"My dear Anita, you are as charming as ever!" Luna laughed.

"Quiet on the com!" Tom snapped. Then he immediately felt bad. *Luna's trying to get me angry so I will not be able to think straight,* the young inventor told himself.

"I hired some of the best scientific minds in the world to make my ships as fast as the *Exedra*," Luna continued. "They've done very well, don't you think?"

Tom flipped the transmitter off and turned to Aristotle. "Plot us a course back into hyperspace. Anywhere within a quarter of a parsec!"

"Computing," the robot answered.

Tom activated the transmitter once again. "So, you've been sitting out here all this time just waiting for me to come back from Alpha Centauri." He tried to put a bantering tone into his voice to match Luna's. "I'm flattered!"

A blinding flash of light suddenly shot across the bow of the *Exedra*.

"Great Scott!" Tom shouted, veering the ship to starboard.

"Those dirty—they're *shooting* at us!" Ben growled.

"By the way, if you're thinking of going into hyperspace, I wouldn't," Luna drawled lazily. "You might say I've been rather preoccupied with hyperspace lately, and I've done some asking around. Even you might not know this, Tom, but with my fleet so close on your heels, if you were to enter hyperspace, your calculations would be thrown off by the magnetic interference from my ships." Luna paused to chuckle. "You might never come out, son!"

Tom quickly glanced at Aristotle. The robot nodded his head, confirming Luna's theory.

Another flash of light zipped across the *Exedra*'s bow, closer to the delicate exterior computer sensors than the first one had been.

"I do not understand this conflict, Tom," said Mok N'Ghai. "Is your planet sending out this David Luna to destroy you? If so, I find it incredible in light of what you have done. You and your friends saved my planet from destruction by the barbarous Chutans. Your planet should receive you as a hero!"

"David Luna does not represent my planet, Commander," Tom explained. "This is a—a private war. Mister Luna heads a multinational corporation similiar to Swift Enterprises. Only instead of inventing things to benefit mankind, as my father and I have tried to do, Luna steals and buys all of his inventions for the benefit of himself."

Tom made a slight adjustment in three of the switches on one side of his computer console, then continued.

"David Luna stole your probe, Aracta, after my friends and I found it on Io, a moon of the largest planet in this system. He wanted the secret of your interstellar drive so he could build a giant space fleet and rule the Earth. We got the probe back and I used what information I could get from it to build the *Exedra*'s stardrive. Luna then tried to steal the *Exedra*, but we left for Alpha Centauri before he could catch us."

Tom sighed in frustration. "It looks like he might win this time, unless—"

Suddenly, the *Exedra* lurched sickeningly and Tom heard a deafening thud that reverberated throughout the ship. The port monitor flickered and then died.

"Damage report!" Tom shouted.

"The port cameras have been hit," Aristotle said. "No other damage was sustained."

"That was too close, you fool," Tom heard Luna growl. The man's voice sounded far away, and the young inventor knew he had not been meant to hear the comment.

"He wants us alive," Tom whispered to Mok N'Ghai. "That gives us some room to maneuver."

"I do not understand why someone from Earth does not intervene in this conflict," the Skree commander said. "Either you or your opponent are bound to be injured or killed!"

"Luna has no respect for anyone's law but his own," Tom explained. "He would not submit to any official intervention and he never honors his promises if a better situation comes along."

Tom closed down the ship-to-ship frequency. "Anita, Kate, and Ben, start firing randomly. Don't shoot to hit, just try to keep them at a distance. I'm going to do some fancy flying. Luna is trying to head us into deep space where he'll have the advantage. I'm going to get us turned around and make a fast run for Earth!"

The indicator lights for the ship's laser cannons began flickering. Tom put the *Exedra* into full planetary drive and fired the attitude jets, sending the ship into a steep vertical climb above the pursuing fleet.

Abruptly, a dot of light on the computer display flashed and then disappeared altogether.

"He flew right into my blast!" Anita exclaimed.

The audio channel between the two ships suddenly sprang to life.

"That was nice shooting," Tom heard Luna say, but the man's voice had changed. It was no longer light and bantering. "I want you and your friends alive because I have a project that needs your skill and ingenuity. However, when you begin to cost me more in terms of time and money than you are worth, I may have to reconsider. I don't like to see red ink in my accounting ledger, if you understand my meaning, Swift.

Don't make me have to cancel your account."

"The outer hull temperature is approaching dangerously close to the maximum tolerance," Aristotle said.

"The fleet has changed formation," noted Mok N'Ghai. "They are going to use the advantage of their greater numbers to prevent you from heading into your system."

"The fighters are just fast enough to do it, too," Tom said with dismay.

On the computer screen, the eight remaining small dots had spread themselves out into a latticework pattern, with the space fortress in the center.

"We could try to go between the formation," Ben suggested. "The *Exedra* is fast enough!"

Tom shook his head. "No good, Ben. There's still enough distance between us so they could see what we're doing and close their formation to prevent us." He hesitated a moment, then went on. "I don't want to try blasting my way through because no matter how good a shot you are, we're still outnumbered. Besides, a lot of innocent people would get hurt. My fight isn't with the pilots of those fighters, it's with David Luna."

"That would never stop Luna if he were in your situation," Ben protested.

"But it's stopping me," Tom said firmly.

The radio crackled into life again. "The fortress sensors indicate that you're having a little trouble with your heat shielding, Tom," David Luna purred. "You're being unreasonable. Let's stop this cat-and-mouse game and talk. If you give up now, you can come aboard the fortress and no one will harm you. You have my word."

"Your word?" Tom blurted angrily. "How much is that worth these days?"

"Then let me put it another way. Be smart and live a little longer!" Luna snapped coldly.

Tom looked at Mok N'Ghai. The alien shook his head sadly. "He's got us, Tom. We really have no other choice. But as long as we're alive, we may think of a way to get out of this!"

"Okay, Luna. Let's talk," Tom regretfully agreed.

The young inventor was aghast at the actual size of the fortress as they drew closer to it. It was a broad, floating city in space!

"How could he have built this thing without anyone knowing about it? It's monstrous!" cried Anita.

"Remember, Luna's main business has been mining the asteroid belt," said Tom. "No one has contested his exclusive rights to that territory because it's not a very pleasant place to be and because it would be unbelievably expensive to battle him in his own backyard."

Kate One Star shook her head sadly. "Besides, asteroid mining attracts only a certain kind of person. Luna's employees are tough, close-mouthed, and he pays them very well. I should know," she added regretfully.

"You mean he's able to buy their loyalty," Anita snapped.

"As much as he can with money," Kate replied evenly. "Remember, money doesn't buy every-thing."

"Fortunately," Ben put in.

"I doubt very seriously Luna has been both-ered with anything like a government inspection since this operation started," Tom observed.

A few moments later the young inventor gave the *Exedra*'s attitude jets one last, brief burst. The starship lightly settled itself into the center of a ring of landing lights that surrounded the em-blem on the surface of the space fortress landing platform. All around them, Tom could see pairs of small fighters landing on specifically marked areas, and he knew their accuracy was impressive.

"Well, we've landed," Anita muttered. "What next?"

A series of loud, booming noises came from beneath the *Exedra*, followed by the clashing of hydraulically driven gears.

"We're going down," shouted Kate, pointing to the ship's front port. The stars were moving vertically upwards.

"We're on some sort of platform elevator and we're being taken into the fortress itself," Tom declared.

The loud noises continued and the bridge of the *Exedra* suddenly went pitch black as the ship sank below the level of the landing platform. Tom could hear the heavy thumping of his own heart. It's just like David Luna to pull a theatrical stunt like this to throw us off guard, he thought.

But he was impressed with the fortress's construction and design.

"Am I imagining things, or are we entering a field of artificial gravity?" Ben asked.

"No doubt about it," Anita replied as she peered through her port. "Whatever this thing is, it's been thoroughly thought out."

Kate sighed. "David Luna never does anything halfway. That's why he's gotten where he is today."

Tom nodded. "That's what makes him such a formidable opponent. I suggest for the time being we all cooperate as much as possible while we keep our eyes open and try to come up with a plan to get ourselves out of here."

The platform bottomed out with a hard jolt. There were more heavy machinery sounds from above and below. Then there was silence.

Five minutes passed in which no one on the *Exedra* spoke and no sound came from the outside. Then an unfamiliar voice spoke over the radio.

"Mister Swift, Chief Engineering Supervisor Parkinson here. Please open your hatch."

Tom flicked the transmitter switch with a finger that felt like lead. "Acknowledged. Hatch cycling."

He turned to his companions and with a heavy sigh said, "Let's get going. We don't want to keep our host waiting."

Tom and his friends walked down to the exterior hatchway in silence. Tom's mind was working furiously. He looked around for something to grab, something to hide somewhere on his person that could maybe aid in an escape. But there was nothing that would not be found in a body search and Tom knew that was the first thing they could expect from Luna.

Anita stepped through the inner section of the hatchway and into the airlock, which was now pressurized for entry. She turned, smiled thinly, then proceeded to the exterior hatch.

Tom pressed a button and the hatchway opened slowly. Light flooded the dim chamber, casting grim shadows off the group. Slowly, the heads, faces, and then bodies of five of David Luna's elite private guard, dressed in crisp, white jumpsuits and white vacu-form boots, became visible. Each had a blaster weapon leveled at the open passageway and its exposed occupants.

A trim, darkly handsome figure emerged from the left and stopped directly in front on the ramp of stairs that had been wheeled into place beneath the hatch.

"How nice of you to drop in," said David Luna, smiling.

Chapter Four

Luna's eyes stared at Tom without expression. "I'll see you alone, Mister Swift, when my men have finished welcoming you to our home. For now, I would appreciate it if all of you would please cooperate with the requests we make of you. It is necessary to take certain precautions out here in space. I am sure you realize that and will follow orders."

With that, the man abruptly turned on his heel and walked to the corner of the corridor. Just before disappearing around the bend, he stopped. "It is especially nice to see you once again, Kate One Star. I was very worried about your sudden and unexpected disappearance from the ranks of my employees." With a cold smile, he added, "I note the uniform still fits you well." Then Luna was gone.

"This way." A guard pointed with his laser pistol.

As they marched along an antiseptically clean corridor to what was probably a prison complex, Anita managed to catch Kate's attention and wink at her. Kate merely raised her eyes to the ceiling, indicating their helplessness.

They halted in front of a door that was guarded by two of the tallest, meanest looking men Tom had ever seen in his life. One of them unlocked it and entered, while the other looked over the group of young people and snarled at them. Then the first guard jerked his head at Tom, signaling they were to go in.

The group walked slowly through the doorway. Inside, the guard ordered them to sit down and wait.

An hour later, Tom was marched back along the corridor and through a maze of elevators and hatches to Luna's private quarters. Finally, the stern-faced guard by his side motioned for the young man to step through a beautifully carved, antique oak door.

The change from the ship's corridors to the plush interior of David Luna's private study was so abrupt that Tom stood openmouthed with surprise. The evil millionaire, sitting behind a large, ornately carved, antique oak desk that matched his door, began to chuckle.

"I'll handle our guest now," he told the guard.

With a solid but muffled sound, the door closed and Tom realized it concealed a sophisticated security hatch.

"Before you say anything, let me assure you that your friends will be treated as honored guests," Luna began. "I merely thought it appropriate that you and I talk together—without the tiresome distractions of lesser people around. Leader to leader, you might say." Luna beamed at Tom like a proud father.

The young inventor bridled at the man's casual dismissal of his friends as "lesser people," but he held onto his temper. It was more important to find out what Luna wanted.

"I trust you've had time to freshen up after your long ordeal in space," Luna said, walking out from behind his desk.

"If you call being searched, having your clothing put into a disintegrator, being tossed into a decontamination shower, and then dressed up like a monkey 'freshened up,' then I suppose the answer is yes," Tom replied coldly.

"I hardly think you look like a monkey. Red

becomes you," Luna said, pointing to the crimson prison jumpsuit and sneakers Tom was now wearing.

"At least I'll stand out in a crowd," Tom noted ruefully.

"My idea exactly," Luna said easily. "The jewelry accent is simple, but effective in setting off the entire outfit, don't you think?"

Tom looked down at the plain metal identification bracelet on his right wrist. It had been fused into a solid piece and was not removable. A chill went through the young inventor as he began to suspect that identification might not be its only purpose. He knew how thorough David Luna could be.

"This way, please," said Luna, as he walked toward a wide archway closed over with smoked glass. The glass slid back with a whoosh of air as Luna approached it.

"Do I have a choice?" Tom asked with mock politeness.

"No," Luna answered. "I'm just being polite. There's really no excuse for bad manners. But in case you're thinking about being so rude as to refuse my hospitality, perhaps a small demonstration is in order."

Luna turned up the cuff of his deep maroon jumpsuit sleeve, exposing a metal wristband simi-

lar to Tom's, except it was much more compli-
cated. There were rows of colored buttons and
several dials on it. It looked, in fact, like the
wristband Anita Thorwald wore to access her
personal computer.

"Now, I'll make this brief so as not to bore you,
because I know you're an intelligent young man
and there will be no need for overemphasis."

Luna pressed a red button.

Tom suddenly felt very happy and rather
weak. There was no pain, no discomfort, but the
will to make any decisions was completely gone.
He was content simply to stand still, grinning
rather stupidly at his host.

Tom's mind fought the strange feeling, but it
was no use. He remained lightheaded and ex-
tremely lazy. Suddenly, he was drifting away on a
soft breeze. He thought he was lying in the sun,
his back feeling the definite sensations of warm
ground pressing against it.

He smelled freshly cut grass. The warm rays of
a summer sun melted any tension from his body.
To move the smallest muscle was simply too
much of an effort.

Abruptly, the overwhelming sensation was
gone! Tom was back in the space fortress, facing
David Luna. He gasped at the notably severe shift
in moods.

"Tampering with alpha waves can produce many different states in a person's mind." Luna smirked. "Some of them much less pleasant! An easy way to control potential troublemakers, don't you agree? Shall we get on with our chat, now that the demonstration is over?"

Tom silently fingered the bracelet on his wrist and nodded.

Luna waited for him to walk through the archway, then followed and palmed a hidden switch. The room was instantly filled with soft, overhead lighting. The same plush vermilion carpet that was in Luna's study also covered the floor and walls of this room. Tom's eyes grew wide with wonder as he stared at the unusual furnishings. Computer games of every size, shape, and variety were arranged in clusters around an enormous banquet table holding plates of hors d'oeuvres.

"Are you expecting visitors?" Tom asked.

"Just you, Mister Swift."

Luna walked to the table, picked up a gleaming white china plate, and proceeded to fill it with food. He motioned Tom to do the same.

"I especially recommend the Hawaiian chicken triangles," the industrialist said, without looking up.

Tom selected one and looked at it suspiciously.

Sensing the young man's hesitation, Luna took another and popped it into his mouth.

Tom bit into the small sandwich and was rewarded with a delicious combination of tastes. He quickly identified chicken, pineapple, and walnuts, but the seasoning was too subtle for him to name. "Fabulous," he commented.

"I'm glad you approve," the older man said. "I like my guests to have a good time."

A large platter of red and black caviar divided by wedges of chopped egg caught Tom's eye next, and he treated himself to a large helping. The egg was real. So was the caviar. Tom had attended enough parties and social gatherings to know the difference between the real items and the synthesized variety one usually found in space. There were plates of avocados stuffed with shrimp, artichokes filled with feta cheese, a Gorgonzola mousse, a moussaka, and what looked like acres and acres of canapés. Tom's mind reeled when he thought of the money all this real food had cost.

Luna poured himself a glass of wine from a carafe in the center of the table and then gestured toward Tom. The young inventor declined politely.

"I'd like a glass of milk, please," he said.

"I'll order it," Luna said, frowning with disgust.

The milk arrived and Tom thanked the attendant. He was getting impatient with Luna, who seemed to be interested only in filling his stomach and making idle small talk. Certainly the man had not sent for him merely to show off his chef's skills or to impress him with his money.

Luna refilled his plate with food, then motioned for Tom to follow him into one of the clusters of games.

"Do you know how to play 'Cosmic Destroyer'?" Luna asked, seating himself in front of a console.

The screen displayed a constantly repeating sample of the game and Tom saw tiny computer representations of starships being chased by what looked like asteroids. Occasionally, one of the ships would be hit by an asteroid and explode. Instantly, it was replaced by another ship. On the top of the screen, the computer flashed the high scores that had been recorded in previous games.

"I'd play a game with you," said Tom, "but I don't have any change with me."

"I'll pay," said Luna.

"May I ask you a question?" Tom quizzed.

"Ask anything you like," the older man said,

searching in his pocket for a coin to begin "Cosmic Destroyer."

Tom gestured around him. "How could you possibly put this whole thing together in such a short time?"

"I had the games shipped here from various Luna Corporation bases," Luna replied. "They make life in the asteroid belt interesting. Nothing exciting ever happens around here, you know."

Tom grimaced. "I'm not talking about the games. I mean this space fortress. It's a remarkable engineering feat. From the little I've seen so far, it's obvious that even all *your* money could not rush the construction of a spaceship of this size and complexity."

"Thank you," Luna replied smoothly. "Coming from a genius like you, that is indeed a compliment."

"This must have been under construction long before our struggle over the alien probe," Tom said.

"True," Luna admitted. "It started out to be my personal headquarters. But as the construction began, I realized there was potential in having something more than just another big spaceship." The man toyed absentmindedly with the coin in his hand for a moment.

Tom decided not to interrupt the silence. Luna

seemed very relaxed and off guard. Perhaps he would slip and tell Tom something potentially useful.

"It made a lot of sense to incorporate a section so my scientists and technicians could be close by," Luna went on. "Easier to keep an eye on them, you know," he added with a sly grin. "Then we needed space to house shuttle ships and mining tugs. Plus accommodations for those working here. Not just the miners and technical people, but security, housekeeping, and all the rest."

The man flipped the coin into the air and caught it easily. "One thing just led to another, you might say. Much of the construction and the plans already underway could be modified to fit into the space fortress, so it wasn't as though we had to start out fresh to build this place. After I obtained the alien probe from you, I decided to change the plans once more and make it—fully operational." Luna smiled at Tom once again, but there was no humor in the smile.

"Then you suddenly ran off to Alpha Centauri! Why did you do that? I had hoped the two of us could have worked out some kind of deal!" Once more he flipped the coin into the air.

Tom reached out and grabbed the coin before it could fall back into Luna's hand. "The fact that you were trying to capture the *Exedra*—and in a most unfriendly fashion—may have had something to do with it," he snapped.

"Ah yes, well, you must have had quite a time there. You even brought back an alien monstrosity!" Luna observed.

"Commander Mok N'Ghai is *not* a monstrosity!" Tom corrected sharply. "He happens to be a very intelligent, very loyal being!"

"Yes, you're quite right. I'll have to speak with him myself." Luna reached into his pocket, got another coin, and slipped it into a slot to start "Cosmic Destroyer."

The machine's display pattern disappeared. Motioning for Tom to sit next to him, Luna grasped the controls. Tom marveled at the look of intense concentration on the man's face as he stared at the screen, waiting for the game to begin. Was it more than just a game to him? Tom wondered.

A ship appeared in the center of the screen, then asteroids began streaking toward it from every direction. Luna fired the guns and Tom was forced to admire his lightning-fast reflexes. Luna hit several asteroids, which broke up into smaller ones and sped harmlessly off the screen. As he maneuvered the ship expertly, dodging and weaving in between the tiny planets, the older man spoke once again.

"I can go into hyperspace to get out of the way of the big ones, like this," Luna said. Not taking his eyes off the screen, he jabbed at a glowing red button on the controls and the small ship suddenly disappeared in a flash of light, to reappear, half a second later, in the right-hand quadrant of the screen.

Unfortunately, it was in the path of a large asteroid and before Luna could turn and fire on it, the ship was struck. It disappeared and a second ship appeared in the center of the screen.

"The trouble with hyperspace is that you have no control over where you come out," he went on.

The man's serious attitude about the game was beginning to bother Tom.

"Yes," Luna continued. "All of these little ships can go into hyperspace at the flick of a button, and here I've spent millions of dollars and hired the best scientific minds in the world, and my one big ship can't go into hyperspace! What do you think of that?" He moved away. "Here, you take over."

Tom took the controls and tried to concentrate on keeping the tiny ship from being hit by an asteroid, but his mind was racing. Luna was finally getting to the point! He wanted the stardrive for his fortress. The young inventor fired the ship's guns and exploded several asteroids in succession. Luna frowned, watching the screen with nervous anticipation.

"You're a good pilot," he muttered. "One of the best."

As Tom continued to keep the ship from being struck, his score was slowly edging past Luna's. He could tell his opponent was not happy with this turn of events. He risked a quick look sideways, trying desperately to figure out what Luna's real game was. Then he lost his ship to an asteroid.

Luna was elated. "This is just a stupid game." The millionaire laughed.

Suddenly, he stood up, towering over the surprised boy. "All right, Swift, fun's over."

He glowered at Tom, who could not help but recoil from the hate and fury radiating from the man who only seconds before had been laughing. Luna's eyes had opened to reveal the evil that he had been carefully hiding with a thin veneer of politeness.

Now he revealed himself as he really was—a ruthless madman, desperate to get what he wanted, regardless of what it might cost anyone else.

His hand went to the silver bracelet at his wrist. "Are you going to play along with me and be partners—or do I show you what other things alpha waves can do?"

Tom looked at the snarling, contorted face above him and tried to think of a way to buy some time.

"You have ten seconds to answer," Luna said coldly. "Beginning *now*!"

Chapter Five

Tom decided on a desperate gamble to try and gain a little time. "May I ask a question?"

The unexpected response clearly took Luna by surprise. He stepped back and looked puzzled. Then he nodded.

"Building this entire operation obviously cost a fortune. You are completely in control of the space fortress and all the mining operations. Yet you were supposedly stripped of all your connections with the Luna Corporation and denied access to its money, resources, or employees," Tom said.

"I don't hear a question," Luna growled.

"How did you do it?" the young man asked.

A crafty look crossed Luna's face. "You're very naive in many ways, Swift. A genius, yes. But you are way out of your depth in some matters. I built the Luna Corporation from scratch. A few policemen and politicians and busybodies millions and millions of miles away aren't going to take it away from me!

"Now, quit stalling for time. I need your answer," Luna insisted, once again glowering over Tom's chair.

"Suppose I do agree to help you," Tom said. "Supplying the stardrive capability to the space fortress is quite a different thing from installing it in the *Exedra*. I would have to know what you've done so far."

The older man seemed to relax just a bit. "I gathered some information from the alien probe before you got it back," he said. "It was only a few details about the Skree and some technical data on the stardrive. But it wasn't enough to really do anything with. I knew the stardrive was theoretically possible. In fact, some of my top scientists had been working on it for a couple of years, but they kept coming up against impossible obstacles."

The man smiled at Tom in a superior fashion. "You might be surprised at the scientists who are on my payroll," he gloated. "Coleman from Harvard, MacCallum from Cambridge, Flynn from Princeton—they've all made their contributions to the Luna Corporation."

He laughed at Tom's expression of dismay when the names were mentioned. "Shocked that such eminent men would forget their principles for a fat check? I told you you were naive. But back to the stardrive." Luna began to pace around the room. "These people came up with their idea of a prototype. It's installed in this fortress, and the plans, the designs, and the technicians all say it should work. Every test but one has been one hundred percent positive so far. And I want to be absolutely certain before I risk the fortress and my life."

He whirled at Tom once again, his eyes gleaming with a strange light. "*You,* young man, are the only human being who has built a stardrive, installed it in a ship, and successfully used it. I want you to tell me if this system will take my fortress through hyperspace successfully."

"And if I won't?" Tom asked politely.

"Then you and your friends will die—except the alien. I have other plans for him," David Luna said matter-of-factly.

"I bet you have wonderful things in store for Mok N'Ghai," Tom said bitterly.

"Well, I suspect he'll be more reasonable about

this whole thing than you are," Luna said smoothly.

"I'd rather die than see you get hyperspace capability for this fortress," Tom exploded. "I know exactly what you'll do with it. You'll enslave all of mankind and anyone else who gets in your way!"

Luna was silent for a few moments. Finally, he said quietly, "But don't you see, Tom, that's not the point."

"Not the point?" the young inventor asked, puzzled.

"No. The point is this: will your friends be willing to die? Will they be willing to sacrifice their lives for your out-of-date code of ethics?"

He leaned forward so his face was almost touching Tom's. "Will your code of honor allow you to sacrifice *their* lives for your ideals?"

Tom knew there was nothing he could do. Besides, he told himself, if he agreed, there might be the opportunity for sabotage and, perhaps, escape. Dead, he would be no good to anyone.

"I'll need help," he said finally. "Let my friends work with me."

"No help!" Luna snapped. "I don't trust you."

"I won't do it alone. I know about the stardrive and I'm the only one who can tell you the truth about the one you have on this ship. You can kill me, but it won't get your fortress the stardrive, will it?"

Tom realized he now had the upper hand and was determined to push for everything he could get while he still had the advantage.

Luna frowned darkly at him. "I warn you, the first sign of any trick on your part—or on the part of your friends, including that dumb robot —and you will answer to me!"

He stood up and turned to a guard whom Tom had not seen enter the room. "Take him away."

"Oh, Mister Luna, you forgot something," the young inventor said.

Surprised, Luna turned around.

"I think this is yours," Tom said, tossing the millionaire the small coin he had snatched from the air only a few minutes before. "I wouldn't want you to think I steal things from my host." With that, Tom walked swiftly from the room— quite satisfied, all in all, with the way things had gone.

Three days later, Tom and Ben were sweating their way through another afternoon, continuing their exploration of the space fortress's master computer.

The machine was so enormous that it occupied

a section of its own in the giant spaceship. However, the crawl space inside the computer was rather limited and cramped. Tom was unable to look at his friend when they talked to each other.

"Hand me the five-thirty-seconds socket, will you please, Ben?" The young inventor held the small access panel in place with one grease-and-dirt-covered hand and stretched the other toward the computer tech.

Ben placed the tiny socket firmly into Tom's palm. "Your scalpel, Doctor," he said jokingly.

"Working on this *is* a lot like performing surgery," Tom said. "Luna told me that he had changed his mind about what to do with the fortress, and the workmanship on this machine certainly shows it. Some of it was done right, but the rest was a crummy job."

"They were obviously in a great hurry to finish it," Ben agreed. "The construction is sloppy and I see a lot of things that were not done properly."

Tom lowered his voice before continuing. "My professional opinion aside, however, the stardrive is very close to working. That scares me."

"We really don't want it to work, do we?" asked Ben, also quietly.

"No. But we have to show some small progress to keep Luna happy—and keep that Engineering

Supervisor Parkinson off our backs. If they get the slightest bit suspicious, we're doomed!"

"It's *Chief* Engineering Supervisor Parkinson. For heaven's sake, get the man's title right," Ben growled in mock horror. "I almost think Parkinson is worse than Luna. He's been watching us like a hawk, just waiting for a mistake that he can show his boss to get us into trouble. His ego is enormous and that makes him a very dangerous man!"

"I agree," said Tom. "We've got to stay out of his way."

Ben leaned close to Tom's ear, pretending to check a circuit board. "Has Aristotle figured out the design of the fortress and where they've stashed the *Exedra*?"

"No, but he thinks he's close. He has to be subtle when he taps into the computer circuits, so he won't get caught."

"Speaking of tapping into circuits, have you noticed how many of these components don't have any identification numbers?" Ben asked.

"I've seen about a dozen designs stolen from Swift Enterprises alone," answered Tom. "Several others are from General Transistor and Diode, and a couple are definitely counterfeit Amalgamated Electronics patents. That's typical for a David Luna project."

"Part of the problem is that some of these components aren't compatible," Ben said. "There's a lot of systems duplication, too. Some of these circuits just aren't necessary."

Tom unfolded part of the computer diagram he had been given and studied it for a moment. Then he pointed to a tiny section of it. "I'm convinced that switch M-89, circuit 459Y duplicates switch M-36, circuit 138W."

Ben peered at the diagram for a moment. "I agree. It must be very confusing to the brain box to get two signals."

"M-89 has more capacity, so let's try cutting out M-36 and see if we can get one strong signal."

"I'll go do it," Ben said. He picked up a soldering iron and a face shield, and was about to crawl past Tom, when the young inventor tugged at his sleeve.

"How's Kate?" Tom asked. "She hasn't said much since we were forced aboard. I'm worried about her. After all, David Luna is a vindictive man and Kate ran out on him once. There's no telling what he might do to her."

"I've seen her this way before, after a rough assignment," Ben said. "It's almost as if she's building up her energy. Unfortunately, she's now being forced to do training exercises with Luna's private guards as a sparring partner!"

"Luna must have something in mind. I guess he hasn't given up hope that she'll work for him again," Tom said.

"He doesn't like losing anything, does he?" Ben's expression grew thoughtful. "How many people are on this space fortress, Tom?"

"From what I've seen, I would estimate it could house about two hundred comfortably. It's severely understaffed right now, though. Are you thinking we should try to fight our way out?" Tom looked at Ben quizzically.

Ben sighed. "No way. That would be stupid. Luna has far too many guards and we don't know where the *Exedra* is—or anything else, for that matter."

"Don't give up hope, buddy," Tom said cheerfully. "We'll get out of this somehow!"

"Yeah." The young computer tech edged carefully past Tom.

"Aristotle! How are you and Anita doing on your section?" the young inventor called out. He began spinning the small bolts on the access plate into place in their proper torquing sequence. The tiny but strong battery-powered ratchet made a whirring sound that echoed hollowly through the vast interior of the computer.

"Everything in the designated circuits of this quadrant has the proper continuity," the robot answered. His voice sounded far away. "Working on this computer has made me appreciate your genius for design," he added.

Tom laughed.

"Don't tell him!" Anita scolded teasingly. "He'll get such an inflated ego that he'll be impossible!"

"Thanks a lot!" Tom said, trying to sound offended but not succeeding very well. "We're ready for another simulation, I think. Will you two go and assist Commander Mok N'Ghai in setting it up while I finish up here?"

"Yes, Tom," replied Aristotle.

The young inventor noticed once again the change in the robot's attitude. Even he was becoming increasingly depressed about having to work on Luna's stardrive system.

Tom rolled over in the cramped space and shook his head. The maze of wires, circuit boards, and access panels extended in all directions as far as he could see. The computer was needlessly enormous.

"Hey! Cut that out!" Ben suddenly yelled. He was somewhere outside.

"I saw you take that apart, young man!" shouted an angry voice that Tom recognized as Chief Engineering Supervisor Parkinson's. "I'm calling Mister Luna! I think you and your friends are trying to sabotage this fortress and the stardrive."

Tom heard a shrill whistle, followed by the thunder of feet running toward the computer. "Guards, arrest this man!" Parkinson thundered.

Chapter Six

Tom's heart leaped into his mouth! It would be terrible if Ben, and possibly all of them, were arrested! Had Parkinson actually seen Ben do something, or was he just bound and determined to get them out of his way?

Quickly, the young inventor crawled out from the computer and rushed toward the sound of the argument.

"What's going on!" David Luna demanded, striding angrily up to Parkinson.

"These kids are trying to sabotage the fortress!" the man answered, with a swagger of authority in his voice. "I personally supervised the construction of this section. Nothing is wrong with it. Yet I caught Walking Eagle ripping some electronics out. It looks like sabotage to me!"

"That's a lie!" said Tom. He turned to Luna and looked at him angrily. "I told Ben to remove a section of circuitry because I felt it needed to be done in order to make the stardrive work. That *is* why you brought me here! I'm keeping my part of the bargain!"

"Someone isn't telling me the truth and there's a way to find out who's lying," said Luna. He very calmly reached for the silver bracelet on his wrist.

"No!" cried Tom. The young inventor grabbed Luna's arm, wrestling with the man to keep him from pressing the buttons.

"Please listen to me," he pleaded. "That's not necessary!"

Luna's guards reacted swiftly. Tom felt himself pulled off the man by several pairs of hands and flung backwards. He hit the computer console hard. The impact stunned him. Dizzy, he reached out blindly to keep himself from falling.

His hands closed on a large, black lever, which suddenly gave way, tumbling the young inventor onto the floor.

"Tom, no-o-o!" Ben screamed.

Tom looked into his friend's face, still slightly

disoriented from the rough handling by Luna's guards. "What's wrong, Ben?" he asked.

"I had to disconnect the fail-safe system to get to the M-36 switch. I was about to reconnect it when *this* guy," he gestured to the confused Parkinson, "interrupted me."

Understanding suddenly flooded over Tom, and his whole body went numb. "You mean the stardrive was just activated? There were no safeguards in operation?"

"Exactly!" Ben said.

Tom knew everyone's life was at stake. Within seconds, the fortress would be shot through hyperspace to an unknown destination. That was assuming the stardrive worked. If it didn't—well, Tom's mind refused to even think about what the consequences would be.

"Everyone down!" he shouted. "Get down on the deck! It's the only chance you have to—"

Suddenly, the world turned inside out. Tom felt sick to his stomach and his head was spinning. The pressure was almost unbearable.

All over the ship, the crew and guards were screaming in terror.

The young inventor searched for Luna in the chaos of terrified, running bodies. He was lying on the deck as Tom had ordered. For the first time, Tom saw real fear on the evil millionaire's face. There was good reason, Tom thought to himself. The fortress was racing through hyperspace—uncontrolled! Then he passed out.

Tom felt the touch of cold metal against his bare skin and awoke with a start.

"Tom—" Aristotle said, hesitating.

"Shhh!" Tom hissed, putting a finger to his lips. Quickly and quietly, he got to his feet, looking around. Everything was quiet. The ship was back in normal space, so the stardrive had at least worked.

But all the humans, and Mok N'Ghai, had blacked out during their hyperspace transit.

They would become conscious again within moments. The young inventor knew he would have to act quickly if he were to gain freedom for himself and his friends.

David Luna was lying on the deck and Tom crept over to him, hardly daring to breathe. If he could just remove the control bracelet and get his group armed before Luna and his men awoke, they had a chance.

The problem was, Luna was lying partially on the arm with the bracelet on it. Tom remembered how Aristotle's touch had brought him awake. He would have to be very careful.

In the background, he heard the first stirrings of people regaining consciousness and knew that he had only seconds to act. As carefully and delicately as he could, Tom grasped Luna's control bracelet and tugged.

Luna came to life without warning and Tom felt his hand caught in a viselike grip.

"I don't know how you managed this," Luna snarled between teeth clenched in anger, "but before you die, I'll find out!"

"I don't know what happened," Tom protested, trying to break Luna's iron hold.

All around him, the young inventor heard sounds of groggy alarm as Luna's guards realized what was happening. Tom swallowed hard in frustration and stopped struggling. He felt the touch of steel at his throat and looked up to see weapons pointed at him.

"What happened?" asked an angry guard.

"Why did we black out?" demanded another.

"You never said anything about this in our contract!"

"I have a wife and family on Earth!"

"Take it easy," Luna warned. "I'm in control here and I intend to find out what happened."

Tom looked around at the anxious, tense faces of Luna's people. They could turn into a lynch mob. He hoped fervently that their fear would not make them violent.

"I honestly don't know what happened," said Tom, evenly. "We apparently entered hyperspace and then—"

"Hyperspace!" shouted someone.

"Where are we?"

"This calls for high-risk bonus money!"

There were grumbles of agreement. Luna held up his hand and an uneasy silence fell on the crowd, which pressed closer around Tom and Luna.

"You all knew that I wanted stardrive capability for this fortress," Luna said. "It seems we have it, thanks to our friend, Tom Swift. Congratulations on a brilliant achievement, Mister Swift."

The young inventor saw that Luna was gaining control of his people again. That was not good. As long as the industrialist was threatened, there might be a chance for Tom and his friends.

"Don't congratulate me yet," said Tom. "I don't know where we are or if the stardrive will work again. We may never get back to Earth!"

The trick worked. The crew began arguing and shouting.

"We'll be stuck in outer space forever if you

lose your heads!" Luna yelled angrily. He turned to Tom and frowned. "If this was a fluke, you'd better find out how to make it happen again."

"Tom! Where are you?" the young inventor heard Anita shout.

He rose to his feet and strode through the crowd, paying no heed to the weapons pointed at him. One man reached out to grab his arm. The young inventor merely looked him in the eye and said evenly, "If you harm me or my friends, you'll never get home!"

The man let go, grumbling fearfully.

Several guards were holding Ben, Anita, Aristotle, and Mok N'Ghai near the computer console. "What's our position?" asked Tom.

"We are three point five one light years from Earth," Aristotle replied.

"We should be near a small system the Skree call Tanue," Mok N'Ghai spoke up. "I was setting up the simulation, as you had instructed, and I arbitrarily picked coordinates that I knew. It's an insignificant yellow star with three very ordinary iron-core planets. They are too far away to be of much use and too damp for my people to colonize."

"Run a check on inertial guidance," Tom said worriedly. "See if you can backtrack our trip through hyperspace."

"Please return to your duty stations," Luna shouted at his crew. "We have work to do. Trust me. I've never let you down before!"

Slowly, the crowd of workers and guards began to drift off. Tom smiled with satisfaction. Luna might have pacified his people for the moment, but the seeds of doubt had been planted. He would have a harder time keeping his crew under control from now on. Tom hoped his enemy would have to work so hard at it, he would pay a little less attention to his captives.

Abruptly, Luna's control bracelet began beeping loudly. The industrialist frowned. "What's the matter?" he asked, pressing one of the buttons. "This had better be important because you're on the priority channel!"

"This is Doctor Cazier. Er, Mister Luna, could you please come to the science level? We've made a—um—remarkable discovery—unbelievable! You must see it!"

It was obvious that the scientist was so excited about something that he could hardly speak.

"You and your friends might be interested in this, Mister Swift," Luna said. "Besides, you've done such an excellent job of feeding the climate of fear among my people that I don't dare leave you with them!"

The small group followed Luna to the science

level in silence. He threw open the door to Dr. Cazier's lab and marched in. After a few steps, the millionaire suddenly stopped in midstride and gasped out loud.

Tom and his friends hurried in to see what could possibly have had such an effect on David Luna.

There, in the center of the lab's main viewing screen, hung a planet like a Christmas ornament! Its many vibrant colors shimmered and glistened, glowing brilliantly against the black velvet of space.

Luna stared at it a moment in silence, then shrugged his shoulders.

"Is this what you called me here for, Cazier?" he barked.

A tall, curly haired scientist detached himself from the group gathered in front of the screen and peered over the rims of his glasses at the industrialist. He seemed puzzled by Luna's reaction.

"This is planet number three," Cazier said. "The sensors went crazy when we picked it up, so we've been concentrating our attention on it."

"It's very beautiful," said Anita. "Is it inhabited?"

"As far as we can tell, there's no intelligent life," Cazier said, happy that someone was taking an interest. "We can't detect any cities or other obvious signs of civilization."

"The land cannot support sophisticated architecture," said Mok N'Ghai. "Sixty percent of this planet is swamp, the other forty percent is ferrous rock with traces of other minerals."

Luna's eyebrows went up.

Tom almost heard the sounds of a cash register as he saw the industrialist's sudden interest in the planet.

"That's why I thought you should know about it," Cazier went on. "It's a—a gold mine, and I mean that literally!"

"Why didn't your people claim the planet for themselves and exploit its resources?" Luna asked, whirling to face the Skree commander.

"There are several reasons," Mok N'Ghai replied. "First of all, the cost of mining and then shipping the minerals back to Kosanth would be prohibitive. There are so many other mineral-bearing planets closer to us, that we can't even mine all of them. There would be no reason to go as far as Tanue. Also, the working conditions here are not suitable for my people. The moisture would cause respiratory problems and mandate the use of suits and artificial environments."

The Skree ambassador paused for a moment, unsure of how to continue. "Perhaps the most important reason, however, is that the Tanue system lies close to the border of the Sansoth Empire. The Sansoth are a fierce people who do not take kindly to strangers settling in their neighborhood."

"You're telling me that the mighty Skree, who have the technology to send a probe all the way to our system, are afraid of the Sansoth?" Luna sneered.

"It is because we are intelligent that we see no need to cause unnecessary hostility," the Skree commander replied evenly, but Tom detected his annoyance. Luna was oblivious to it.

He whirled to look at the planet again. "If I claim this gem of a world for the Luna Corporation, I can exploit its resources as I please. Why should I waste my time bickering and bargaining with the authorities on Earth about taxes, labor relations, safety inspections, and quotas when I can have a planet of my own with no authority but mine?"

"Why, indeed?" said Tom sarcastically.

Luna fixed the young inventor with a triumphant grin. "Now that I can zip in and out of hyperspace as I please, there is no one to stop me—except *you,* Tom Swift. You and Swift Enterprises are my only competition."

"We don't know if you can zip in and out of

hyperspace," Tom said. "But, then, you can always become king and sole proprietor of your own planet if things don't work out!"

"You really don't understand some of life's little subtleties, do you, Tom? Wealth and power are only enjoyable when they're recognized. What fun could I possibly have ruling a planet millions of miles away from Earth if I couldn't get back there occasionally? You must remember the old saying, 'If you've got it, flaunt it!' "

"That's the most twisted philosophy I've ever heard!" Ben declared. Luna did not comment.

Instead, he turned back to gaze at the planet. "You know, it reminds me of my mother, Genevieve Luna. She was a lot like that planet—beautiful on the outside, with a core of iron. In fact, I think I'll name my planet after her. *Belle Genevieve!* I like the sound of that! Now, while I'm occupied with laying claim to my world, you can solve the problem of getting us back to Earth, Tom!"

"What if I refuse?" the young inventor asked.

"Are we back to that again?" Luna sighed.

"It seems to me that we have a choice of dying now or dying later, but you're still going to do away with us when the time is right, aren't you!" Anita said angrily.

"Except, perhaps, for you, my dear."

Anita made a sound of disgust and turned her back on the man.

"What about the Sansoth?" asked Tom.

"I'm not worried about them. This fortress can withstand any assault. And now, if you'll all excuse me, there's work to be done."

Luna turned to the curly haired scientist. "How long before we can go into orbit around Belle Genevieve, Cazier?"

"Approximately twenty-two hours, sir."

"Good. By that time, I hope you'll have our problem worked out, Tom."

Don't get your hopes up too high, the young inventor thought to himself. I'm tired of your game of cat and mouse—especially since I'm the mouse! Anita is right. Whether it's now or later, you're still going to get rid of us when it suits you! So far, you've been manipulating me because I keep my word, but the time for being a nice guy has passed.

The young inventor turned his head and caught Ben looking at him intently. He smiled at his friend and began softly whistling a tune which he knew the young Indian would recognize. It was "Dixie."

Chapter Seven

Two days later at lunchtime, Tom picked up a tray and a sterile, disposable utensil packet from the rack, then shuffled forward in the long line of employees waiting to get into the fortress's central mess hall. With a deliberate show of boredom, he casually looked over his shoulder to make sure that Kate One Star was still behind him.

Luna had been keeping the young woman separate from her friends, and Tom suspected it was because the industrialist felt they would be helpless to plot anything without her. This was the first time the young inventor had seen her in the four work shifts that had passed since the discovery of Belle Genevieve. Apparently, in all the confusion and excitement, someone had made a mistake in scheduling.

The line was moving slowly but steadily. Ahead, Tom could see a computer monitor with the day's menu displayed. As usual, there was quite a selection. Roast beef, vegetable chow mein, and spaghetti with meatballs were the main entrees. From past experience, Tom knew that the meat was real, not the dehydrated soy substitute that was usually served in space. The luxury-loving Luna worked his people very hard, but no one could say he did not take care of them.

The delicious odor of hot food was being wafted to Tom's nose by the ventilation system. He had to admit that one of the most beneficial results of Belle Genevieve's discovery was that he and his friends were now eating in the central mess hall instead of in their quarters. Expeditions were going to and from the planet at all hours and the fortress was constantly short of personnel. To economize, someone had ordered their guards reduced to the minimum, which meant there was no one to maintain continuous care of the prisoners.

Tom smiled to himself. That was just fine. He had given no outward signs of rebellion, yet his mind had been working overtime, plotting and planning an escape. He had silently observed the routines of the fortress, noting every weakness, every inconsistency, and had finally devised a plan.

Kate One Star picked up her tray and slowly walked up behind Tom.

"I was in a practice session today," she whispered without moving her lips. "Luna's people are really scared. There's a rumor going around that we'll never see Earth again. Is it true?"

"Maybe," said Tom, but he winked at the young woman. Several people around them stopped talking and looked in their direction. Tom pretended that he had not noticed.

When it was his turn, the young inventor got a generous helping of spaghetti, a large tossed salad, milk, and a piece of cherry pie, then walked over to join Ben, Anita, Aristotle, and Mok N'Ghai at a table.

The mess hall was crowded, since the work shift was changing and there was an overlap of people eating. It was the period when Tom and his friends preferred to eat because things were always disorganized and noisy, so their conversation was less likely to be overheard.

"We've been so worried about you, Kate!" Anita exclaimed, as the young woman put her tray on the table and sat down next to Tom. There was a lot of room around them, not only at their table but at the tables nearby. The other workers stayed as far away from Mok N'Ghai as possible. The seven-foot alien was the focus of frequent suspicious, hostile glances, even some belligerent stares, but there were also a few looks of appraisal and curiosity.

Kate smiled at Anita and then glanced at the guard standing near the exit door. The smartly uniformed woman coughed and then looked away deliberately. Tom noticed it and raised his eyebrows questioningly.

"I still have friends among the guard," Kate said.

Tom nodded. "Well, whatever you do, don't show any reaction," he began, speaking just loudly enough for his friends to hear. "Aristotle just located the *Exedra*! He has been checking each section of the ship by scanning its contents on the official manifest in the computer. The only problem was the fortress is so huge that he could only check one or two sections at a time for fear someone might catch him tampering with the computer."

"Where is it?" asked Ben, not looking up from his plate.

"Parked on David Luna's private hangar deck,"

Tom replied. "I think we're about ready to attempt breaking out of here. I tampered with the long and short range scanner circuits while I was working on the stardrive computer—or, at least, while everyone thought I was working on it. Power is fed to the indicator lights on the control console, but the fortress is effectively blind. That should buy us some time before our escape is discovered."

"Speaking of discovered, here comes trouble," Anita warned. "There are some guards walking toward us."

"It would be wise to cooperate with them," said Mok N'Ghai. "We are definitely the object of their attention."

"Tom Swift?" inquired a burly man, obviously the one in charge. The other two guards casually spread themselves out until the three had the table surrounded.

"I'm Tom."

"You and your friends are scheduled to be transported to the surface with the next shift. Mister Luna's orders. Two of the fighters got bogged down in the mud and all extra personnel are being taken to the site to help out. Mister Luna will be supervising the operation personally."

"What about Commander Mok N'Ghai?" asked

Tom. "Belle Genevieve is too damp for him and—"

"Mister Luna made no exceptions," the guard replied, his impassive expression slipping as he gave Mok N'Ghai an undisguised look of loathing.

"But—" Tom protested.

"It is better not to argue with them, Tom," the Skree commander advised.

"Listen to your bug friend, fella," the guard said nastily. "Now move it!"

The shuttle to the surface was a small ship, not much more than a space taxi. Tom recognized it as a standard Workman-Six, with beefed-up landing gear and some flotation pods welded to the exterior. It would not be big enough for effective cargo hauling.

They were pressed in behind a metal screen, which was locked across the chamber, separating the passengers from the two guards and the pilots. Tom quietly motioned to Aristotle to stand next to the screen. He could see the readout screens and would know when they had dropped away from the mother ship and had flipped over to descend to Belle Genevieve.

Tom was counting on the robot's lightning responses. He pressed his knee against Anita's and indicated she should alert Kate, Ben, and

Mok N'Ghai. With his eyes, Tom signaled Kate to take care of the guards. Cautiously, she began to gather her legs under her.

Then Tom quietly moved his hand next to the quick-release buckle on the seat strap, the only thing that kept him from floating around in the gravity-free cabin.

They entered the planet's atmosphere and the cabin began to heat up. The refrigeration unit and the heat deflectors worked hard to keep the temperature down, but it was a losing battle.

Tom heard one of the pilots muttering to the other, "These quick drops save energy but, boy, do we get to fly a sauna!"

Tom watched the screens. The curve of the planet flattened as they dropped lower. At about 50,000 feet, he whispered to Aristotle, "Rip out the screen."

The robot's powerful arm was already in motion, a silvery blur through the air as he pushed through the stout security screen as if it were made of soda straws. Ignoring the guards, Tom thrust himself through the opening, twisting in the null-gravity to hit both of the pilots across the back of their heads with a flying block. They slammed forward,—unconscious.

Behind him, Kate was demonstrating to two startled guards what her numerous opponents had learned long ago—that she could move with great speed and deadly efficiency. The first guard slammed against the hatch, the foot in his chest propelling her toward the other guard.

His laser came up, but it never fired. Kate struck him across the forearm, then blocked a blow and hit him twice, once on either side of his neck, before he fell.

Actually, he didn't "fall" but drifted around the cabin, a limp collection of arms and legs, until Anita tied him to a seat. Then she bound the first guard into another seat, while Ben pulled the two pilots over so the others could watch them.

Tom was already in a pilot's seat, reprogramming the landing sequence. Suddenly, an alarm light flashed and the ship twisted violently. "They rigged the computer to show any deviation in landing patterns," Tom exclaimed, desperately trying to regain control.

Ben slipped into the copilot's seat, checked everything, then pulled a screwdriver from a wall kit, and began unscrewing an access panel. "More than one way to do this," he muttered.

"Meanwhile, we are back in the flight path to the base camp," Mok N'Ghai said.

The radio crackled alive. "Nice try, Swift." David Luna's voice mocked them. "Don't know how you did it, but I thought you'd figure out something. Too bad, though; I'm one step ahead of you. Stop giving me trouble and get down here. There's work for you." He laughed nastily as the connection broke.

"How are you doing, Ben?" Tom asked.

Ben's head was in the control console and he waved a hand toward the tool kit. "Give me a pair of needlenose pliers." Anita handed him the tool as Tom ran a security check on their air supply.

"Is there anything I can do?" Tom asked. "Or Aristotle?"

"Uh-uh. It's simple enough, but there's only room for one in here. I'm trying to disconnect the exterior control. I just hope our kindly captor doesn't have this booby-trapped. One of these little black boxes could be a bomb."

"Thanks," Anita said dryly. "I needed that."

Tom turned to Kate. "You knocked them out fast enough."

She shrugged, then grinned. "I knew practicing in null gravity at *New America* would come in handy!"

Tom looked out the port. A huge, pale green sea was below them. It looked shallow. A hothouse ocean, he thought, with no depth to soak up the sun's energy. The green is probably algae.

A string of islands appeared on the horizon and slowly came toward them as the ship curved around the planet, slowed down, and descended. Then came a green land mass, thickly jungled, with rugged mountains along the western shores.

Lakes. Jungle. A patch of high desert. The glistening of an immense swamp. Rivers. Another range. They were low enough now for him to get the sense of the forest: great gnarled trees like knotted ropes, as big as office buildings, bursting with dark, green leaves.

Ben heaved himself out of the console, trailing two wires. "Ready?" he said to Tom. The young inventor nodded and put his hands on the banks of buttons. Ben touched the two wires together.

There was a spark followed by a flash and the ship lurched to port. Tom righted it, but there was another sparkling flash from within the console and the ship twisted again, the metal protesting with a loud groan, as the shuttle fought to follow the computer's program.

"Tricky, tricky," Ben muttered, and dived into the bowels of the console again. "I'm trying to connect old-fashioned wires to chips that weren't designed to be used that way."

The horizon was almost flat. Tom could see a vast swamp ahead. Somewhere in that was the base camp.

Anita peered down at the swamp and frowned. "That does *not* look like a nice place," she said.

"You study understatement?" Kate asked wryly, "or is it a natural gift?"

Ben popped out again. "Once," he said. "It'll work maybe once." He ducked back in and called out. "Ready?"

"Ready!"

The ship lurched again, and again the alarm sounded. Tom's fingers punched out a stabilizing pattern, then his hand grasped the joy stick. He angled the shuttle to port, trying to get it out of the immediate area of the swamp, but something snapped.

An explosion made a soft pop and sent a shower of sparks over the console. Then the engine shut down.

The shuttle dropped like a rock. Tom thumbed a button quickly. The engine fired, just enough to lift them over the nearest patch of gnarled trees. From a branch, something shot a pinkish tendril up at the ship, but they whipped by.

Then the engine quit again.

They had no time to do anything but brace themselves.

They hit the black water hard, bounced high, flipped over, fell with a thunderous splash, and flipped over again.

The shuttle skittered across the surface like a

rock, until an airfoil dug into the water and they began pinwheeling wildly. Tom was ripped from his seat and bounced off Anita. They both smashed into the padded walls.

The wrecked spacecraft started to sink, but there was a hillock of slimy dirt under the nose. After a few moments, it settled in the mud.

The passengers untangled themselves. Ben unlocked the emergency exit. Explosive bolts shot the entire airlock off.

Frantically, Tom and his friends tugged at the unconscious guards and pilots, pulling them from the wrecked shuttle. They splashed through ankle-deep water toward a patch of higher ground and deposited the crewmen on the grass.

"Let's get a survival kit," Tom said and turned back. But the shuttle quivered, rolled slowly onto its back, and sank. It settled with an airfoil sticking up, muddy and twisted.

Mok N'Ghai made a thin, whining noise and Tom looked around to see what was wrong. Rising from the mud and brackish water was a great, alien monster!

Chapter Eight

Ween! Ween Ween!

It came from the small head of the huge, long-necked beast. Tom blinked. The sound was not something he heard, but something he *felt!*

"It's telepathic!" Ben gasped.

The body of the swamp creature was massive, something like the ancient Terran Brontosaurus. But Tom had the feeling that, unlike the Brontosaurus, this one was not a vegetarian. The long neck arched, mud dripping and black water glistening along its length.

Ween! Ween! Ween!

Kate One Star stepped forward.

"Get back," Tom ordered. "You don't have

weapons and maybe this thing doesn't come up on land."

Kate reluctantly agreed, and they pulled the slowly recovering crewmen toward the center of the small, grassy island. But the creature lumbered up after them. Its lower legs had thick, stubby flippers, and the long tail whipped back and forth viciously. It snapped a tree trunk in two without even slowing down.

"I'll try and head it off!" Kate said, dashing out before Tom could stop her.

She ran to the right, then reversed herself, darting back, but the swaying head of the beast followed her. Tom saw at least two rows of small, sharp teeth.

Then the long neck plunged, the head striking like a snake at the small human.

Kate One Star did a backflip, narrowly missing the snap of the swamp monster's teeth.

Ween! Ween! Ween!

The thoughts of the great, dinosaurlike creature cut through their minds like a siren. Anita gasped and fell to her knees. Mok N'Ghai stood rooted to the ground, his whole insectoid figure quivering.

WEEN! WEEN! WEEN!

That must be how the creature immobilizes its prey, Tom thought. Then he blinked as he saw

Aristotle lumber forward. Kate was still tumbling about, running back and forth, but she did not have much ground to use.

The robot seemed unaffected by the telepathic assault of the monster. He walked right up to the creature, who apparently did not even see him. It struck at Kate, giving her a glancing blow with the side of its neck. She fell, hitting her head against something, and lay still. The monster raised its head, a hiss coming from its mouth. It prepared for the final, fatal strike.

Weeeen! Weeeen! Weeeen!

Then Aristotle hit the beast.

It twisted in agony, its head swinging and searching, but it seemed incapable of even connecting the metallic robot with the source of its pain.

Aristotle hammered two more iron-fisted blows into the side of the creature and the mountain of wet flesh flinched.

WEEN! WEEEN! WEEEEEEN!

With a groan and a splash, it slipped into the water, shook itself, and sank below the surface. In a moment, all they could see were the ripples as the swamp creature swam away.

Ben sat down in the grass with a sigh, but bounced right up again. He looked down. "There are *things* in there!" he said indignantly.

"Tom," Mok N'Ghai said suddenly. His quivering had stopped, but his claw shook as he pointed to the west. Two dots were coming at them. In seconds they could make out the helicopters. One stayed high, with weapons trained on them, while the other landed to pick them up.

Tom looked around at the swamp stretching away in every direction. "Come on," he said wearily, and led the way toward the helicopter.

He stopped to let Aristotle get aboard. "That was very brave of you," Tom said. "Thank you."

"Oh, no, Tom. When I saw how that thing was affecting the rest of you, I searched the electromagnetic spectrum, isolated the telepathic communication, and shut it off from my receptors. It was really the only way the poor creature could detect anything. As far as I was concerned, it was blind. It was not courage at all."

"Thanks, anyway," Tom said. "Now get aboard."

It was dark when they reached the base camp. Emergency floodlights had been hastily rigged to illuminate the scene of the disaster.

The air was heavy with mist, and the smell of rotting vegetation and warm, damp soil. The light shining through the moist atmosphere was soft and eerie. Tom saw the two fighters lying in a still, murky pool of water. Above it hung the drooping branches of nightmarishly twisted and gnarled trees. Several had their trunks snapped off about midway, casualties of earlier attempts to pull the fighters out of the mud.

All around them, the swamp was alive with strange creatures. Tom could hear chirping, thumping, swishing, and scratching from the thick vegetation that surrounded the pool. The soggy bank was marked by many different kinds of nonhuman tracks. One in particular dominated the others and Ben Walking Eagle knelt down beside it, tracing the outline with his finger.

"This was made by a heavy, bi-pedal carnivore, I think," he said. "See the large depression in the center and four smaller, shallower depressions surrounding it?" The young Indian computer tech pointed.

"Grazing animals usually don't have claws as big or as sharp as meat eaters. I'd hate to meet this critter face to face!" Ben put the palm of his hand over the center depression and spread his fingers as wide as he could. The tips just barely touched the bottom of the smaller pads. "I'd say this animal stands at least as tall as a human," he concluded.

"Your powers of observation are remarkable," said Mok N'Ghai.

"Look at this," Anita cried, squatting down

beside Ben. She dug into the mud and pulled out what looked like a piece of broken pottery. She handed it to Tom and began probing the mud again. Soon she found another smaller piece.

The young inventor stole a glance back at the shuttle to see if their findings had been noticed, but the crew was still busy unloading equipment from the cargo bay. He looked closely at the fragment. It had a hard black glaze on the outside, and it was about an eighth of an inch thick. The inside had a smoother, cream-colored glaze.

"What's your analysis?" asked Tom, handing the fragment to Aristotle. The robot did not reply right away. Instead, he used his sensors to analyze the piece of pottery.

"The ground around here is covered with this stuff," said Anita, holding up several more of the odd pieces.

"Doesn't the broken pottery show that there's intelligent life on this planet?" Kate asked.

"I do not remember any mention of it in our records," Mok N'Ghai said. "And our explorations are usually pretty thorough."

"These are not pottery fragments," Aristotle spoke up. "They are organic. I believe they are egg shells."

Mok N'Ghai gasped, but before he could say anything, a burly work-shift supervisor shouted at them.

"Let's move along!" he said, motioning to Tom and his friends wearily. He was wearing a white uniform similar to the crimson ones the young inventor, Anita, Kate, and Ben had been issued —heavy jumpsuit, boots, gloves, and visored cap insulated with some sort of fiber-fill material. But the man's suit was no longer white. It was stained brown with mud, and he looked exhausted. "Mister Luna has orders for you," he added slowly, as though each word were an effort.

Tom looked out over the swamp. A shiver of excitement went through him. What kinds of life existed in the ecology of Belle Genevieve? The tracks in the mud and the egg shells were only the first clues in that mystery. The young inventor's curiosity made him want to go off into the wilds of the planet and explore. That was not possible now, though, and he doubted that they would see any of the creatures for a while. It seemed that the humans and their equipment had scared everything into hiding. Reluctantly, Tom moved toward the supervisor, motioning for his friends to follow.

"It looks like two space jockeys tried to land on soft ground going too fast and overshot their mark," Tom said to the supervisor when he came closer. The young inventor pointed to the deep furrows that the ships had plowed in the mud before crashing into the pool. "I only hope no one was injured. That's a pretty bad smash-up!"

The man grunted. "The pilots escaped with minor cuts and bruises, fortunately. The ships were overloaded with equipment and the men were too inexperienced at moving cargo to compensate for the extra weight and ground conditions. They're just fighter pilots—young kids at that!" the supervisor finished angrily.

"Not everyone is a great seat-of-the-pants flier, as you are, Tom," said Aristotle.

Tom blushed.

"None of us expected to have to do this kind of work," growled the supervisor, whose name tag read G. GUNN. He was big and burly, with freckled skin and reddish blond hair. Tom could see, from the blisters and red spots on the man's hands, that he was not used to hard manual labor.

Gunn caught Tom looking at him and laughed self-consciously. "I'm a design engineer, and I spend most of my time in front of a computerized drafting table," he said. "But duty calls, as they say. Actually, this would be okay if it wasn't such back-breaking work. Cazier and the science boys are all excited, that's for sure. They're sick of developing weapons systems for the fortress. I don't blame them. None of us really likes working on a war machine."

Tom quickly stepped to one side as a land rover, which had been hastily converted to carry cargo, crawled by, its treads digging up the mud and throwing it in huge, wet globs. "Why do you work for Luna, then?" he asked the supervisor.

"It's a ride into space, and the only one most of us here are likely to get." Gunn looked straight into Tom's eyes, and the young inventor saw envy in the man's expression. "My folks have a small farm in the Midwest. I had to put myself through school. I've wanted to go into space since I was a kid, but if you don't know the right people, and you don't have the right degrees from the right schools, you have to wait for your big break. This was mine," he said, gesturing broadly.

"You're wrong about that," said Tom. "Working for David Luna isn't any kind of break!" Then the boy heard a dry, hollow-sounding cough behind him and turned to look at his friends.

Mok N'Ghai had dropped a few paces behind the group and was trying to suppress a cough. Tom was worried about his health. There had been no protective clothing on the fortress for a seven-foot insectile, so an outfit had been improvised for him using the fiber-fill material and pieces of the alien's own suit. But it was not sufficient. The Skree had a cold and was already walking stiffly.

Gunn turned to follow Tom's gaze. "We've heard rumors about him," he whispered. "It's hard to believe that anything that looks like him could be intelligent!"

Tom shrugged and did not answer. It was not difficult to see Mok N'Ghai through this man's eyes. After all, he and his friends had had to conquer their own instinctive reactions to the insectile Skree. But things were different now, and mankind was going to have to adjust to aliens.

Their boots made squishing sounds in the trampled mud as the young inventor and his friends followed Gunn into the base camp. It was crude, but it was a foothold on the planet's surface. Tanue was dipping below the horizon and its sunset of glowing orange, yellow, and soft red left Tom thinking briefly of Earth. Would he ever see it again?

Chapter Nine

"You may wonder why I've asked you here," said Luna, striding up to Tom confidently.

"I certainly was," Tom replied dryly.

The lean and muscular industrialist was accompanied by two of his guards. They did not seem to be part of the ground crew. They were clean. Tom doubted that the older man ever went anywhere without the protection of guards.

Gunn excused himself and, with a brief look at Tom and his friends, marched off to join another work crew.

"In that disgusting pool of water, you saw two of my fighters," Luna went on. "Normally, I would write this accident off the books and allow the wrecks to continue sinking into the quagmire —which they are doing hour by hour. Unfortunately, those two fighters contain several important pieces of seismographical equipment that I need to begin exploiting this planet's resources. So far, all attempts to rescue them without your rather unique inventive genius have failed."

Tom could see that. The broken trees, the trampled mud, and the exhaustion of the work crews spoke all too clearly of the previous efforts.

"This sure must seem like paradise to you, Luna," said Kate One Star.

Tom saw a brief flicker of rage in the industrialist's eyes. It was quickly suppressed. Control was David Luna's secret of success.

"The wreckage is sinking at the rate of two centimeters per hour," Aristotle commented. "Will the equipment be ruined if water enters the holds?"

"The sooner you work this problem out, the faster we can all get back to the safety and more comfortable conditions of the fortress," Luna said in reply.

Tom thought for a moment. "What's needed here is something to increase the torque—or pulling power—of a simple winch. I see that you've already tried using a block and tackle arrangement, but the trees aren't strong enough for a brace." His voice trailed off as he continued to search for something.

"There!" he cried suddenly, pointing to the rover standing nearby. "You have a three-speed vehicle. That means it has a transmission with gears in it. We can use the gears to multiply torque."

"That's a priceless piece of equipment," Luna protested. "Use something else!"

"I thought you brought me down here for my ideas," Tom said calmly. "That's the best one I can come up with."

The industrialist growled. "Use anything you want," he conceded. "Just get those ships out of the mud!" With that, he stalked off.

Several hours later, Tom wiped his grease-covered hands on his jumpsuit and looked at the crew Luna had assigned to help him. They were sagging in various postures of exhaustion. Some of them had been working for eighteen hours straight.

He saw a few people checking their watches, and knew that the shift change would be occurring soon. A transport would be sent from the fortress, and a new group would replace some of the people. But Tom and his friends would not be among those going back.

He picked up the one-and-a-half-inch combination wrench he had been using on the drive mechanism of the rover and idly balanced it in his hand. If only there was a way out of this desolate wilderness!

Nearby, Mok N'Ghai tried to suppress another cough. Tom frowned. Breathing had become difficult for the alien and he would not be able to tolerate the climate on Belle Genevieve much longer. But being transported to the planet's surface had really wrecked the plan for escape that Tom had so carefully thought out and shared with his friends. Would they have another chance?

In the distance, the young inventor saw that much progress had been made in the construction of the base camp. Since his arrival, a frame had been erected for the main dome, the floor had been laid, and the work crews were now spraying the outer shell with a plastic compound. When dry, it would be as hard as concrete.

Disciplining the workers was becoming a problem, however. Everyone stopped work more and more frequently to look skyward, hoping to catch the first glimpse of the shuttle that would take them back to the fortress.

"You're wasting time!" Luna shouted at Tom. He left a cluster of engineers and walked briskly over to the young inventor. The ever-present two guards caught up with their boss, and then lolled wearily against a discarded piece of the rover.

"You're wrong," said Tom, suddenly bringing up the box end of the wrench. It caught Luna under the chin and sent him flying backward. He fell to the ground—unconscious!

There were grunts of surprise from the guards but, as Tom had hoped, everyone was just too exhausted to react quickly.

Kate and Anita jumped one of the guards and took his blaster and helmet. Anita quickly tossed the blaster to Tom, who pointed it at the unconscious industrialist.

"That just goes to show you don't always need a plan," said Ben, smiling at Tom. The young Indian computer tech reached for the other guard's blaster. The man gave it to him without a struggle.

"If nobody moves, Mister Luna won't get hurt, you have my word," said Tom.

Nobody moved.

At least Luna's employees had some sense of loyalty, Tom thought to himself. Or perhaps they just had a strong sense of survival. He remembered what Gunn, the work-shift supervisor, had said. Everyone wanted to get back to Earth. Without Luna, they might not make it.

Luna was beginning to regain his senses. As

much as he hated to do it, Tom put the muzzle of the blaster against the older man's cheek. "Don't make me have to use this," he said evenly, trying to hide his nervousness. From now on, the timing would be critical. He did not know how long he could hold Luna and he *had* to hold him until the shuttle arrived.

"I—I understand," Luna said. The words were not very clear. He had a nasty-looking purple bruise underneath his chin and his jaw was beginning to puff up.

"The shuttle will touch down in approximately ten minutes and seventeen seconds," Aristotle reported.

"Put the radio out of commission," said Tom. He did not want anyone to get the heroic idea of alerting the shuttle to the situation on the ground.

Ben hurried over to the base camp communications equipment. The young Indian motioned the operators away from it and then fired a series of short blasts at it with the weapon he had taken from Luna's guard. Metal and plastic melted and burned. Sparks shot into the air from the guts of the radio.

Luna spat a mixture of saliva, blood, and chipped teeth onto the ground and chuckled, but there was no humor in it.

"The shuttle will want landing confirmation," Kate said worriedly.

"Aristotle can take care of that," Tom stated.

The seconds seemed to crawl by like hours while everyone sweated in silence, even though the air was chilly and damp with mist. Once, the young inventor made eye contact with Gunn who, like the rest of the workers, stared at him and shifted restlessly from foot to foot. Tom could not read the man's expression and he wondered how long he could continue to hold everyone using Luna as hostage.

From the direction of the pool, thick bubbling sounds could be heard as mud began flowing into the holds of the wrecked fighters. Luna swore under his breath.

Then a dull whine, accompanied by a shrieking sound, cut through the tense silence. Tom looked skyward and saw the bright glow of the shuttle's fusion nozzles. With great relief, he watched it descend onto the landing markers and settle heavily into the mud. Using Luna as a shield, Tom motioned to his friends. They backed slowly away from the crowd of workers and moved toward the craft.

The first worker out of the shuttle walked several feet before realizing that something was wrong. She froze, not knowing how to react.

"Just keep going and no one will get hurt," Ben said, motioning with the blaster for her to join the others.

When everyone had debarked, Ben, Anita, and Kate hurried over to stand next to Tom. The young inventor watched, alarmed as Mok N'Ghai moved slowly forward, aided by Aristotle. The alien was walking stiffly and Tom could hear him wheeze with every step. Quickly, Anita, Ben, and Kate helped the insectile into the shuttle.

Tom looked at the workers. Some faces showed fear, others suspicion. "I'm sorry, but you'll all have to wait until the next shuttle to get back to the fortress," he announced when his friends were inside. "If we get to the *Exedra* safely, we'll radio in your situation. As for the fortress space-drive, I've rigged it so it will work once more. Don't try to follow us because you have only one chance to get back to Earth. I didn't want this fight, but losing it means losing my life. I'm very sorry you all became involved," Tom concluded.

"What will you do with me?" asked Luna, sneering. "You won't be able to keep me a prisoner once you get to the fortress! Admit it, Tom—your situation is hopeless!"

"Is everything ready?" Tom shouted through the open doors, ignoring Luna's taunts.

"We're waiting for you," Anita replied.

Tom looked at Luna, and for the first time, he smiled at the industrialist. Luna's eyes narrowed with suspicion and fear. Suddenly, the young inventor gave him a hard shove. The older man staggered a few feet forward, then fell face down into the mud.

Luna sprang to his hands and knees quickly, but Tom had already jumped inside the shuttle. The doors snapped shut and sealed with a click and a thud. Several workers ran forward and dragged the enraged man away from the landing markers as the shuttle's drive whined to life!

Chapter Ten

During the brief trip back to the fortress, Tom quickly outlined his escape plan to the others.

"That's awfully risky," Anita said. "Isn't there some other way for us to get into the *Exedra*?"

"We don't have time to sit and map out an alternate strategy," Kate insisted. "Tom's idea is simple and has a good chance of working. Besides," she added, "we do have the element of surprise on our side."

"That's right," Ben put in. "The last thing those guards in the fortress will be expecting is us marching in like we own the place!"

"Prepare for docking," Aristotle warned.

"Okay, everyone. This is it!" Tom called. "If 107

you ever wanted to be an actor, this is your big chance."

Tom's strategy was to pretend to be in charge of the prisoners. He and Kate would act as guards, wearing the helmets they had taken from Luna's men on the planet. He was hoping that everyone would be tired from the long hours spent working on Belle Genevieve, and that because of Luna's absence from the fortress, security would be a bit relaxed. But he did not dare count on it!

"Let's go!" he said, opening the door to the shuttle.

As he had expected, the bay crew only gave them the usual stares of revulsion and curiosity that the seven-foot insectile alien and the gleaming metal robot always elicited from the fortress personnel. The group marched without incident to David Luna's personal hangar.

The huge deck was cavernous. Tom heard hollow echoes of footsteps in the background. There was moderate activity and he hoped it would be enough for cover.

He stepped up to the officer in charge of the deck, whose I.D. tag read SANDRA CARLSON.

"We have orders from Mister Luna to take these prisoners back to their ship," Tom said.

"The bug is sick and the robot needs recharging."

He forced himself to look bored with such a routine task, but he could not keep his gaze from wandering to the *Exedra*.

The ship appeared as though it had not been touched. However, there was no way to tell for sure. He would have to make a thorough check once he got inside.

One glance at the stern face of Officer Carlson, however, and Tom knew that boarding the *Exedra* would be difficult.

Ms. Carlson unclipped a small communicator from her belt and punched for a tie-in with the ship's main communication center.

"What's your name and classification number?" she asked suspiciously.

The young inventor felt himself begin to sweat hard under the woman's penetrating gaze. He automatically turned to his "fellow guard" for help.

Kate One Star's face was totally hidden by the full battle helmet she was wearing. She stepped away from her friends, drawing attention to herself, and nudged Mok N'Ghai forward with a grunt and a jab of the blaster she held against his side.

"Well?" asked Carlson, impatiently ignoring Kate's attempted distraction.

"Somebody probably forgot to notify you," Tom said. "We've just come from the surface and, er . . ." He knew the woman would catch him if he lied.

Suddenly, Aristotle waved his arms in the air and made a whining, machinelike sound. "This does not compute," the robot said, using a very mechanical voice.

Tom was as much taken by surprise as was the supervisor, but he recovered quickly. Aristotle had never done anything like this before, but there had to be a reason for it. That much the young inventor knew for sure.

Aristotle began walking toward the supervisor, stiff-leggedly.

"Help!" she yelled.

She drew her blaster, but did not fire. Instead, she backed away from the crazed mechanoid.

Without warning or apparent purpose, Aristotle turned and went toward a group of workers who seemed to be frozen in their tracks with fright. One of them suddenly came to life and drew his blaster. He fired at the robot, and a beam of pure energy ricocheted off Aristotle's mainframe and struck a bulkhead. A red burn mark appeared and cooled to carbon black.

"Stop that, you fool!" Carlson shouted. "You might depressurize the deck!"

"Let us pass," said Tom. "We can straighten out the paper work later. First, we have to get that robot recharged!"

Aristotle picked up a large metal box and turned it upside down. Tools clattered onto the deck. Then he threw the box at a maintenance worker who was trying to get out of the way. Tom noticed that it fell short of its target. The robot had missed on purpose.

"Do something!" the supervisor screamed, as Aristotle headed toward some cargo modules droning over and over, "I must fulfill my programming! I must fulfill my programming—"

"I don't know," said Tom, sounding doubtful. "He's out of control now. You'd better let me take charge temporarily!"

"Get him aboard the ship, before he wrecks the whole deck," yelled Sandra Carlson.

Aristotle appeared not to have heard her, but Tom noticed that he changed the direction of his path of destruction and lumbered nearer to the *Exedra*.

Anita reached the outer hatch first, and began cycling the lock. Ben, Kate, and Commander

Mok N'Ghai were right behind her. The supervisor's eyes narrowed and she frowned thoughtfully. Tom followed her stare and saw that a lock of red hair had worked itself out of Anita's cap.

Before the young inventor could think of an explanation, his attention was diverted by the sound of the main lift. The door opened and Chief Engineering Supervisor Parkinson stepped onto the deck. "What's going on here? he shouted.

Tom walked briskly toward the *Exedra*, ignoring the question.

"Wait a minute," Parkinson yelled, charging forward. "You're Tom Swift!"

Tom broke into a run.

"You'll never get out of here! You're trapped!" the supervisor screamed.

Tom reached the hatch of the *Exedra* and climbed through behind Aristotle, who was trying his best to hurry. "Thank you for the flaw in your logic circuits that made you cause that diversion!" the boy panted. "It's just what we needed!"

"It was not a flaw, but rather the perfection of your programming," the robot replied. "It enabled me to make the logical decision to behave illogically."

Tom sealed the hatch and patted the mechanoid on his metal chest. "I'll want you on the bridge," he said. "We may need more of that logical illogic to get out of here!"

Kate and Ben were watching the chaos on the hangar deck through a front port. Tom rushed onto the bridge and dived into his acceleration couch.

Luna's employees were firing their blasters at the ship and Tom could hear the bursts of energy crackle against the hull. He was not worried, however, because he knew any weapon that was safe to use inside the space fortress was not powerful enough to harm the *Exedra*.

"Parkinson is right," Kate said worriedly. "We can't open the hangar doors ourselves and Luna's people certainly aren't going to do it!"

"We can't open them *safely*," Mok N'Ghai said as Anita was helping him strap down in his couch. Suddenly, she gasped in alarm, and Tom turned to see what was wrong.

He looked closely at the Skree commander and noticed patches of what looked like green mold growing on the surface of his skin! Mok N'Ghai self-consciously put a hand to his face, and Tom saw that the mold was growing on his fingers and arms, too!

"It was the thing I most feared about the dampness on Belle Genevieve," the alien explained.

"Is there a cure for it?" Anita asked.

The Skree shrugged. "The disease spreads very rapidly throughout the entire body. When it reaches the vital organs, death follows."

"When we get out of here, I'll go into the lab and find a cure," Tom promised.

During their captivity on the space fortress, he had been worried, annoyed, and angry at David Luna, but he had never felt the almost immobilizing rage he now did. Mok N'Ghai's life was in danger because of the evil man and that was intolerable!

Tom fastened his acceleration harness and went through his pre-launch checks. Behind him, everyone followed his example.

"What's the plan?" Ben asked, watching Tom's brow furrowing with intense concentration. The young computer tech could always tell when his friend had an idea that would be risky. "Whatever it is," he added, "we're behind you a hundred percent!"

"Get to the battle station at the forward laser and wait for my signal," Tom ordered. Then he switched the com control over to the exterior broadcasting mode. "Attention, all hangar deck personnel," he said, a deadly calm in his voice. "You have exactly four minutes to evacuate the area and open the hangar doors. After that, we're blasting our way out of here!"

The reaction of the crew below was instantaneous. They backed away fearfully, then turned and ran toward the lift.

Parkinson began to shout at the crowd. Tom and his friends could not hear what he said, but they saw that the workers paid no attention to him. Furiously, the superintendent turned to the ship and shook his fist at it. Then he strode angrily to the elevator.

Thirty seconds passed. A minute. The hangar doors did not open.

"Go ahead, Swift!" Parkinson shouted over the com. "Try blasting your way out! That'll finish you all for good. The hangar deck is pressurized and once you make even a tiny hole in it, you and your ship will be sucked into space and come out in a million pieces!"

Chapter Eleven

"Will we survive the depressurization?" Kate asked Tom.

"It'll work if we can make the hole big enough," said Tom. "There will be damage, though. Both to us and the fortress. I'm surprised that Parkinson's hatred for us goes that deep."

"If we surrender, we're dead ducks," said Ben. "I'm casting my vote in favor of your idea, Tom. The *Exedra* will make it!"

"Commence firing at point-blank range on the widest dispersion setting," Tom ordered.

A beam of intense bluish-white light struck the

hangar doors, but Ben widened it. The beam became softer and covered an area bigger than the ship. It would take a long time to burn through, but the larger hole would do less damage to the *Exedra*.

"Be careful not to let the center heat up too much," Tom warned. "We want the metal to melt evenly."

The doors glowed reddish orange, then yellow. Drops of liquid metal started to flow in rivulets onto the deck.

"Stop!" Kate One Star cried suddenly, pointing to the deck's computer monitor.

HANGAR DECK PRESSURIZED had disappeared from the screen and DANGER—DEPRESSURIZATION IN PROGRESS took its place.

"I didn't think you would go through with it," Parkinson growled over the com. "You've won this one! I won't risk the fortress just to get you. There'll be another time!"

From somewhere deep underneath the ship, Tom and his friends felt a strong vibration and heard the heavy clang of hydraulically operated locks being released.

ZERO PRESSURE flashed onto the monitor and the doors slid open.

Tom activated the *Exedra*'s attitude jets and

maneuvered the ship expertly out into space, where he fired the main drive. On the main screen, the fortress rapidly shrank as Tom called on the *Exedra* for maximum planetary drive speed.

"You'd better go and pick up your boss," Tom radioed back to Parkinson.

There was no answer from the fortress.

As soon as they were a safe distance from the fortress, everyone went to the lab to find a cure for Mok N'Ghai's strange ailment.

They clustered behind Ben, who had done a series of metabolic tests on the Skree commander, and scanned the computer screen as graphs and words flowed across it in a logical, progressive sequence.

"The green mold is a kind of scab," Ben deduced. "Something like the white corpuscles in human blood."

Anita spoke up. "White corpuscles are like cops, aren't they? Any sign of trouble in the body and they come running!"

"Uh-huh. The mold is Mok N'Ghai's body's way to keep away whatever is bugging him." Ben grinned sheepishly and shot a guilty glance at the Skree, who waved a bony hand in negation.

"I'm sorry we don't have time for conventional research," Tom apologized to the alien.

"I understand, Tom. You are the captain. I will follow your orders."

Tom blinked. *Captain* Swift? he thought. Well, he supposed he was, but to him a captain was someone much older.

"We've already tested Mok N'Ghai for allergies," Kate said. "Could we have missed something?"

"It's possible," Tom replied. "Alien physiology is an unknown field to us. All we can do is go by our standard procedures. But I think we can approach this problem on an electronic level."

Ben's eyes lit up.

"Remember the ancient ionizers?" Tom asked the Indian computer tech.

"Sure. They gave a negative charge to air particles, cleared out dust and stuff, and a lot of people thought they made you feel pretty good, too."

"Let's try something like that," Tom suggested.

"Are you going to put Mok N'Ghai into one of those sterile rooms?" Kate asked. "He'd be a prisoner. Alive, maybe, but a prisoner just the same."

"No, nothing like that," Tom assured her. "Here's what I have in mind. Aristotle?"

"Yes, Tom?" came the prompt reply.

"You can help us on this. Interface with the

ship's computer, will you? That'll speed things up so we won't have to translate every little thing into computer language."

"Of course, Tom."

"Now, here's my idea," Tom said, and they all leaned forward.

"How does that feel?" Tom asked.

Mok N'Ghai's mandibles opened slowly, then closed again. "Wonderful," he said. "Rather flat, but wonderful, just the same." The hoarseness was already gone from his voice.

"It works," Anita exulted as they all looked at the little black box slung from Mok N'Ghai's belt.

"Yeah, but *how* does it work?" Kate asked.

"Let me see if I have it right," Anita said. The beautiful young woman had connected her own computer into the *Exedra*'s and had been in on the entire inventive process. "Tom has ionized the air around Mok N'Ghai. He's sanitized it, that's why it tastes flat to him. *Nothing* is getting through to his lungs except the air. It can't. The particles suspended in the air that give him the allergic reaction are charged negatively. Not just dust, but everything. All the spores, anything at all organic."

"He'll starve!" Kate exclaimed.

"No." Tom laughed. "It only affects free-floating material, pollen, dust, spores, things like that. Remember when you tried to shove two magnets together on the like poles when you were a kid?"

Kate nodded.

"Mok N'Ghai is positive; all that other stuff is made negative. You can shove organic material close, but nothing can drift close," Tom explained.

"You have saved my life, Tom," Mok N'Ghai said. "I shall not forget this. The code of the Skree warrior clans will not *let* me forget, of course," he added, making a peculiar sound in his throat.

"Forget it." Tom blushed. "A little black-box wizardry, is all. Anyway, it gave me an idea for another invention. I've been wondering what could be done about the nausea that always accompanies a jump into hyperspace and I think I've solved the problem."

The young inventor went over to his electronics workbench and held up a thin wafer of special plastic. Sections of its upper coating had been removed to expose a layer underneath. The pattern looked like a maze. "This is my mask—or model—for a special circuit that I plan to interface into the stardrive computer." He thought for a moment before continuing. "It will be photographically reduced to macroscopic size and then printed on silicon, like any other chip. But this one's special. When the stardrive circuit is activated, this will cut in and reverse the polarity of all the *Exedra*'s instruments." Seeing puzzled looks, Tom explained, "It creates a temporary pocket of normal space inside the ship!"

"I'll start the photography right away," Ben cried excitedly. "I can have the chip done in no time!"

"Your inventions are truly remarkable." Mok N'Ghai was awed. "You have given my people a passport, not only to your world, but to many worlds with your ionizer. And now you have solved one of the nagging problems hyperspace travel has always caused. I am proud to be your friend and compatriot!"

Tom blushed again.

"One moment," Aristotle said, cutting into the conversation. He was still connected with the ship's computer. "The space fortress is being attacked, Tom. Ships are headed for Belle Genevieve as well!"

Chapter Twelve

"Who would attack—" Tom started to ask Aristotle, but all at once he knew.

"The Sansoth," Mok N'Ghai said, voicing the young inventor's thought. "I feared as much when we first found the strange fragments in the mud of Belle Genevieve. I believe those were the shells of Sansoth eggs. The planet must now be part of their empire, and one of their hatching grounds."

"Eggs?" Anita asked. "You mean that's how they—er—have children?"

"Does your race not reproduce in this way?" Mok N'Ghai asked, his mandibles clicking in amazement.

"Not exactly," said Anita. "I guess we all have a lot to learn about each other!"

"If Luna and his people are still on the planet, then they're helpless against the Sansoth!" Tom said. "We've got to go back and rescue them!"

"Why?" asked Kate One Star. "David Luna is our worst enemy! I say good riddance to him! He's only getting what he deserves!"

"Not quite," Tom said. "When we escaped from the planet, Luna and a lot of innocent people were stranded down there, but with the understanding that they would eventually be picked up and get back to Earth. I personally deactivated the fortress's scanning equipment so that we wouldn't be followed." He sighed. "That is what left the fortress open to a surprise Sansoth attack!"

"Tom—" Ben started to interrupt his friend, but Tom cut him off.

"If I let myself be satisfied by this kind of revenge—or any kind of revenge—then I'm just as evil as Luna! Besides, I have nothing against his people and they have nothing against me. If Luna ever gets what's coming to him, it should be by his own stupidity and vileness, not because I sank to his level. Whatever it costs, we've got to go back!"

A brilliant, burning white light filled the *Exedra*'s main viewscreen. Tom shut his eyes against it, but even then, rainbow-colored dots continued to swim in front of him.

"Another fighter has disappeared from our instruments entirely," said Aristotle. "There is no debris."

Tom opened his eyes. Ahead of them, space was indeed empty around Belle Genevieve. Tom and his friends watched helplessly as fighters from Luna's fortress attempted to take on the attacking Sansoth fleet. The odds were hopeless. The fighters were no match for space cruisers and they had to stay close to the fortress to protect it well. One by one, they were being picked off by the blitzkrieging Sansoth.

"They have disintegrator rays!" Ben said.

"Just give the word and Kate and I will start blasting away!" called Anita over the com.

"No!" said Tom. "They'll focus their disintegrator rays on us and we may not get the chance to at least talk to them!"

"They are not acknowledging our signal yet," Aristotle reported. "I do not think they are in the mood to talk."

"Allow me to try," Mok N'Ghai said. "I have been hesitant to interfere, since you are the captain of this ship, Tom. But they may listen to me."

Tom agreed, then turned to the robot. "Aristotle, you'd better give the battle computer its head now. We don't want to get caught off guard," he said. Aristotle nodded and suddenly the ship swerved sharply and increased its speed. A disintegrator ray passed harmlessly underneath.

"That was one of the best ideas you've had all day," Ben said dryly.

"It's so frustrating to be shot at and not be able to defend yourself," Kate mumbled.

Mok N'Ghai talked into the microphone in a language that Tom did not recognize. It took a few moments for his TTU to catch up with a translation.

"Are you speaking in Sansoth?" Tom asked.

"No. It is Unispeech, a synthesis of several tongues in this sector of the galaxy. It is considered the language of diplomacy," the ambassador replied.

"We have nothing to say to you, violators of the nest!" came an angry, sibilant voice from the radio. "Surrender, murderers of the young, and we will be merciful!"

Tom looked questioningly at Mok N'Ghai.

"The Sansoth are very hot-tempered and tend

to overreact to anything that threatens their eggs," the alien explained. He spoke into the mike again. "I am Commander Mok N'Ghai. I am Skree and I speak for the humans. If your nests were violated, it was unintentional. Call off your attack!"

"Have the Skree become killers of hatchlings, then? And who are these humans?" The radio sputtered.

The *Exedra* increased its speed suddenly, throwing Tom and his friends deeper into their acceleration couches.

"That one almost got our tail," Anita reported.

"Have the Sansoth become barbarians who shoot while they are talking terms?" Mok N'Ghai asked pointedly.

"The Sansoth do not negotiate with invaders and monsters!"

"The humans are neither invaders nor monsters! There has been a mistake. If the Sansoth have become so unreasonable that they annihilate without question anything that moves through their empire, then this incident will have grave consequences among the other civilized peoples of the galaxy!" Tom could tell that Mok N'Ghai was furious. "I am a special envoy on a peace mission to Earth and I speak for my planet Kosanth, and all the Skree! The humans are our allies and if you threaten them, you must answer to us!"

There was a noticeable pause. "We have no wish to offend the Skree with whom we have come to the peace table many times," the Sansoth finally acceded.

"I knew that would get them," Mok N'Ghai whispered in heavily accented English. "Their ships wouldn't fly without certain Skree-manufactured parts, and the rest of the civilized galaxy wouldn't trade with them if we didn't!"

"What?" asked the Sansoth, irritably.

"I was merely conferring with the humans," the Skree replied in Unispeech. "They wish you to let them proceed to the planet's surface unmolested so that they can see the situation for themselves. If any humans have destroyed your eggs or your hatching ground, they will make amends."

"You may proceed," the Sansoth said.

Everyone on board sighed with relief.

A few moments later, the *Exedra* landed on Belle Genevieve and Tom led the way out of the ship. He and his friends stopped—stunned at what they saw.

"What happened here?" Tom exclaimed. "Where is everybody?" The young inventor stared with disbelief at the planet's surface where the base camp had existed only a few short hours ago. It was a scene of devastation beyond the wildest imagination. "Did the Sansoth do this?" he asked Mok N'Ghai.

"This is not their style," the alien replied thoughtfully. "However, we will shortly be able to ask them." He pointed beyond the *Exedra*.

A large ship was coming down out of the sky, a bulbous vessel of distinctly organic design. Tom stared at it, drinking in every detail. It looked as if it had been grown in metal.

"A whole new type," he said in amazement.

The vessel settled down, its shape blending well into the swampland growth. When nothing seemed to happen for several minutes, Tom started looking around at the camp.

He kneeled down to pick up a piece of plasti-foam lying in the mud. The main dome of the camp had been almost complete before their escape. Now it was reduced to a mere fragment of its foundation. Huge chunks of the hardened outer covering were strewn all over the area. Containers of supplies had been ripped open. Coffee, protein powder, dehydrated vegetables, and soya granules had been trampled into the mud. The machinery that David Luna had spent hours transporting to the surface had been destroyed, ripped apart as though it were made of paper. Some of the metal parts had even been crushed flat by some unknown and frightening force.

Koosh-shhhh!

The hydropneumatics of the Sansoth ship's hatch swung it open. After a few seconds, out came several members of the crew.

Anita could barely suppress a giggle. "They look like stuffed toy lizards," she whispered to Tom.

Tom stared at the five bronze-scaled aliens walking toward them on powerful hind legs. He did not quite agree with Anita's description. To him, they seemed more like man-sized, flesh-eating dinosaurs! Their big jaws were lined with double rows of sharp, wicked-looking teeth and he could not tell if they were smiling or hungry. That made him edgy.

The leader of the party stopped suddenly and kneeled down, tracing the outline of something in the mud with a delicate, sharp-clawed finger. "Torith," he said to the others, drawing out the "th" sound into a hiss. They nodded in agreement.

"That's the track I showed you when we first landed on Belle Genevieve!" Ben whispered excitedly. "They're all over this area. The animal that made them must be called a torith!"

The five aliens marched up to Tom boldly, while Kate One Star slowly moved into a fighting stance next to him. One delicate hand fell lightly onto the butt of her blaster weapon, where it rested casually.

Mok N'Ghai cleared his throat—or at least that was what it sounded like—and stepped forward. "We are honored that the captain of such a mighty Sansoth ship would come to talk with us," he said. "It is my privilege to introduce Tom Swift, the captain of the Earth ship *Exedra*."

Tom took a step forward and extended his hand. The aliens did not move, but instead stood looking at him. The young inventor slowly lowered his hand, feeling awkward and embarrassed.

The Sansoth captain blinked slowly. The movement reminded Tom of an alligator lounging in the sun. The alien's uniform was slightly different from those of the rest of his crew—if one could call a fancy weapon harness a uniform —and the young inventor suddenly felt self-conscious. He was sure the Sansoth had noticed his own blue jumper bore no designation of rank.

"I don't think this is going very well," he muttered to Mok N'Ghai.

"On the contrary," the Skree said. "It is only

out of respect that the captain has shown no outward sign of emotion. If he had moved, it would have been to kill us all!"

"Great," Ben whispered.

"This will be an interesting addition to my study of alien cultures," said Aristotle.

The Sansoth captain inclined his head slightly in the robot's direction. "Of what purpose is this piece of equipment that speaks?" he asked slowly.

"He's—he's—" Tom frowned in deep concentration. Did Aristotle really have a purpose? "He's my friend and a vital member of the *Exedra*'s crew," the young inventor finally said.

The five Sansoth looked at one another with expressions that Tom interpreted as extreme surprise. Then the captain narrowed his eyes. "You humans are strange beings if you consider this machine your friend," he said. "I do not know where your planet Earth is, but I hope it is far from here!"

Ben grunted in indignation.

Suddenly, a low groan of pain came from some bushes at the edge of the wrecked camp. It sounded human.

Without hesitation, Tom ran toward the sound and discovered Gunn, the design engineer, lying on the ground, bruised and bleeding from several bad cuts.

"Easy, man," Tom said, gently turning him over and supporting his head so that he could sit up. "You're among friends now!" The engineer looked up and smiled weakly as everyone, including the Sansoth, gathered around him.

"H-how long have I been unconscious?" Gunn asked. Then, feeling the warm sunlight for the first time, he added, "It's been hours, hasn't it!"

The Sansoth captain stepped forward and pointed a finger toward the destruction of the base camp. "What explanation have you to offer for trespassing upon a sacred hatching ground of the Sansoth people?"

Gunn stared at the reptile openmouthed. Mok N'Ghai shifted his feet nervously.

"What explanation have *you* to offer for injuring this man without cause?" Tom countered, fixing the Sansoth with a hard stare.

The captain blinked and his eyefolds arched in frank surprise. "We did not do this!" he declared.

Tom suddenly remembered their use of the disintegrator rays and he believed the reptilian warrior.

"There are torith tracks in the mud," the Sansoth continued. "Some are large and there are also smaller ones. It is my opinion that the beings in this camp encountered a family pack of torith. They are very fierce and there are many on this planet. They cause us much grief."

"Whatever they were, we were fighting for our lives before we knew what hit us!" said Gunn. "They were big, slimy, froglike things with huge claws. There was nothing we could do but run!"

"Did everyone escape?" Tom asked quickly.

"A lot of them did," the engineer answered. "A few of us stayed to fight, but it was hopeless. Those monsters weren't afraid of anything. The last thing I remember is one of them putting its big paws around me. Phew, what a stench!" he added.

One of the other Sansoth spoke for the first time. "This human is a trespasser!" he told the captain. "What are your orders?"

"You know, there aren't exactly any signs around here that say 'Property of the Sansoth, keep out'!" Anita spoke up. "How can anyone know that this planet is your hatching ground?"

"The Skree should have known," blustered the captain.

"And I *would* have known if you had properly filed your claim to this planet with the Council of Worlds!" Mok N'Ghai stated. "I suggest that you call off your attack on the space fortress before you overstep your authority and endanger your claim."

"Registration is pending," the Sansoth captain

grumbled. Without another word, the five reptiles turned abruptly and stalked off toward their ship.

Tom stared at Mok N'Ghai with frank admiration. The Skree had actually gotten the Sansoth to back down, saving all their lives!

"What about Mister Luna and the others?" Gunn spoke up worriedly. "We've got to find them!"

Chapter Thirteen

An hour later, Tom felt as if he had been walking through the swampy land for days. The clump of grass in front of him looked solid enough, but when he stepped on it, his foot sank into mud up to his ankle. Something gray and green slithered off into the water. Tom eyed the next tuft of grass carefully, stepped over to it, then hopped quickly across to a relatively dry section.

Looking back, he watched Ben follow the same route, skipping from tufted island to hummock and passing over the green-black waters. Behind Ben came Kaneth, the Sansoth captain. After

further discussion on the alien ship, he and his

crew had offered to join in the search for the missing humans.

He traveled across the treacherous, deceptive swamp with an ease that the humans envied, and strode as casually along as Tom might stroll down a street on Earth.

Ben, who was breathing heavily, caught up to Tom. They watched as Kaneth avoided the sudden strike of a pink-mouthed water snake, stepped across the last hummock, and passed the two humans as if nothing had happened. The boys exchanged looks, shrugged, and followed the alien.

"I wonder how Kate and Anita are getting along with their Sansoth?" Ben asked, eyeing a cluster of wiggling rats scooting out of their path.

Tom shrugged. "They didn't want us to go with them," he said. "I guess they meant to prove their independence."

"Are you kidding?" Ben exclaimed. "Kate could wipe the deck with us and Anita probably could, too. When we get back, I'll spend more time studying *jeet kune do* just to stay even!"

Kate One Star and Anita Thorwald had gone off in a different direction, while Mok N'Ghai had stayed behind with Aristotle to coordinate communications and to try to contact the fortress as quickly as possible.

Tom and Ben caught up with the big reptilian officer at the edge of yet another stretch of dark swamp water. The lagoon rippled with unseen life just below the scummy surface. The Sansoth scanned the area. "That way," he said, pointing a clawed hand.

The going was easy for a while, curving along the lagoon's shore, and the boys had a chance to converse with the warrior.

"Why did you pick *this* place for a hatching ground?" Tom asked, blinking as a stick revolved itself into a sunning snake and wiggled off.

"Tradition," the Sansoth explained, his bulbous eyes inspecting the smaller humans with a certain aloofness and disapproval. "We are an ancient and noble race. The old ways die hard."

"What old ways?" Tom skipped past a brooding red spider the size of a football inspecting its broken web where Kaneth had walked through it.

At first, he thought the Sansoth was not going to speak, but finally the scaly warrior responded. "Only the strongest must survive. It is our tradition. There are many tests that nature and our people have devised."

They crossed over a narrow stream, sluggishly emptying itself into the lagoon. "Our home world was a formidable place," the Sansoth added.

"Was?" Ben asked.

Kaneth hissed in a way Tom assumed was some kind of sigh. "The Sansoth have been tamed. It is only in the outer worlds, the new worlds, that the proper conditions can be found these days." He stopped, looked up, and watched the lazy flight of some leathery-looking birds with long wings. "The torith are egg-eaters," he said, his grinding teeth making audible clicks. "But they are part of the pattern here to test our descendants, so we cannot kill them."

"But an egg cannot defend itself," Ben muttered.

Kaneth ignored him. "We kill the vermin we call the tor-ocka, instead. They are greater tests because they kill the torith." He seemed to get a good deal of satisfaction from the thought of killing tor-ockas.

"And that leaves more torith to eat the eggs," Ben said. He looked at Tom. "Same story back on good old Earth. They used to have bounties on wolves because they thought wolves were dangerous to humans and ate too many deer. What they didn't realize was that wolves didn't usually attack people, and that the only deer they killed were the sick and old, thus keeping the herds up to only the best creatures."

Kaneth glared at them. "What are you saying? Not to kill the tor-ocka? You humans! Silly, weak creatures!" With a snort, he strode across a low spot, his feet kicking up dirty water.

Suddenly, the scum-clogged surface of the lagoon heaved and broke into a green splash. Something scaly and enormous rose out of the swamp, dripping mud and tangled roots. It shook itself like a wet dog, sending black water and great gobs of stinking mud in every direction.

It roared, a thunderous spasm of sound that froze the two humans in startled fright. All Tom saw was gleaming rows of teeth, a wet, red mouth, scales and claws at the end of stubby feet. It looked like an alligator crossed with a wet bear—*and it wanted Tom for dinner.*

Ben took a step backward, tripped over something, and fell with a splash. Tom turned to help him and felt the wind of a barely missed blow.

A second roar came, but this time it was from Kaneth. The big reptilian warrior stood on one of the tree stumps, pulling something from his belt. His hard claws worked at a tube, unfolding it. There was a metallic click and a curved blade appeared at one end. The Sansoth snarled, his teeth gleaming as he plucked at the baton he had unfolded. Another blade clicked into place. Kaneth was holding a short-handed, double-bladed battle axe!

He launched himself at the swamp beast, teeth bared in defiance, his axe swinging in the sunlight. The creature batted at him with a clawed paw but missed.

Kaneth clung to the scales of the animal, which was easily twice his size. His axe bit deeply into the armored body. The swamp thing cried out and threw itself backwards, taking Kaneth along.

A tidal wave of stinking water washed over Tom, tumbling him into the swamp next to Ben. The two humans jumped up, wiping several leechlike insects from their clothes, and stared at the battle.

"Is—is that a tor-ocka?" Ben asked nervously.

Tom did not answer. Fascinated, he stared at the swamp monster thrashing in the lagoon. Claws and axe gleamed in the sun. The creature roared and Kaneth roared back.

Tom's laser was in his hand, but he dared not fire. It was impossible to see anything definite in the turmoil. The creature cried out, jerking and twisting loose, rising swiftly, spraying gobbets of mud. Kaneth fell back limp and disappeared into the brackish water. The swamp creature turned toward the two boys, its jaws working. There was blood dripping through the caked mud.

Tom raised his laser to fire, but before he could do so, the creature swayed. It let out a surprisingly weak cry and took a short step. Then, it was as if imaginary strings holding it up were suddenly cut. The huge beast toppled back into the lagoon with an enormous splash.

For a moment, neither Tom nor Ben moved. One clawed hand of the creature opened and closed. Then it lay still. It was finally dead! Tom came out of his trance.

"Kaneth!" he cried, wading forward quickly. They found the big Sansoth beneath the shallow water, but pulling him free of the clinging mud was not easy. It took both of them to wrestle him over to the nearest hummock of grass.

"He's still alive," Ben said.

"Call for help," Tom urged, as he attempted to close the warrior's wounds.

"On the way," Ben said, after making the call. His toe touched something hard in the water and he jumped. When nothing happened, he probed for a moment and brought up Kaneth's battle axe.

"Ingenious," he said, studying the weapon. "Primitive, but very useful. Look, Tom, the handle telescopes and locks from this short hand section. The blades are sectional, fanning out and interlocking."

"Looks like the Sansoth come prepared," Tom observed. He caught a movement out of the corner of his eye. "Ben," he muttered, "I think we're being watched. From the trees there, to my left."

"Correct," Ben said quietly. He pretended to take some practice swings with the axe, turning his body with each blow. "Got 'em," he said with a grin. "I think they're our missing friends. At least they looked human."

"Don't scare them off," Tom warned. Stepping up to the highest point of the hillock, he called loudly, "Don't be afraid! We're here to help you! We came to take you back to Earth."

His answer was a rock, which spun through the air, passing only an inch from his head.

"No, wait!" Tom yelled, but more rocks were hurled his way.

"Go away, Swift!" a voice called out. "You're the one that got us into this!"

"It's a trap, Perk," another voice yelled from a spot in the alien forest.

"Get outta here, Swift!"

"No, listen," Tom insisted. "We captured the fortress. David Luna's power has been broken. We'll take you back to Earth—"

Ben jumped up and tried to speak, but a hail of tree limbs and small stones drove him down again. He rubbed ruefully at a bruise. "I always *thought* sticks and stones would hurt you," he quipped.

Tom called out again. "Listen, I'll prove it to you!" He took out his laser and held it at arm's length, then dropped it into the thick grass.

"Ben, stand up, get rid of your weapon," he said.

"Oh, no!" Ben said. But he stood, unholstered his hand weapon, and dropped it conspicuously.

Then they waited.

Kaneth rumbled something and moved, but nothing else stirred for several minutes. "Tom," Ben said quietly, "suppose Luna is out there with them? That's guy's so tricky that—"

"Hey!" came a shout from the trees.

"Yes?" Tom answered.

"We're coming in, but don't you pick up any weapon, hear?"

Tom nodded. He stepped back even farther from where he had dropped the laser. "How's Kaneth?" he asked his friend.

Ben looked up from where he was scraping mud from his boots and trousers. "His eyes are open."

"I am alive, small Terrans," Kaneth said in his

rumbling voice. His forked tongue flicked out, snaring a bright yellow insect that had landed on his sleeve. Then the tongue curled back and the Sansoth's eyelids half closed.

Tom watched a small, ragged band of humans come out of the trees and wade across to the hillock. Their eyes were wary and suspicious. Their only weapons were crude clubs made of broken limbs and a few rocks. Two of them wore the dirty remnants of white laboratory coats.

A young man retrieved Tom's laser while a woman hunted through the wet grass until she found Ben's gun. They did not point them at anyone, but kept them in hand.

"I'm Perkins," a tall, dark, shaggy man said. "I am Mister Luna's downside foreman on this project. Where is he?"

"You don't know?" Tom frowned. "We're looking for him, too." The young inventor quickly filled them in on everything that had happened. Although they listened intently, their eyes were on the Sansoth warrior. He stared back impassively.

"And you, what happened to you?" Tom asked.

Perkins shrugged. "We were going along, then all of a sudden, these—these *things* came out of nowhere and wrecked everything." He waved at the swamp. "We've been hiding out in that—that mess ever since."

"Tom," Ben said, "the other Sansoth are here. They don't look happy."

Tom turned to see nine alien warriors marching steadily toward him, weapons in their hands!

Chapter Fourteen

The leader of the approaching Sansoth made a sharp gesture. All but two of his warriors moved out in a line, weapons at the ready. Those two splashed through the water to Kaneth's side. No one spoke as they briskly examined him, then one of them pressed a bulb to a patch of scaly hide and there was a soft pop.

The Sansoth doctor—or whatever he was—tossed aside the bulb and stared intently at his leader for several moments. Tom sneaked a look at the dirty, bedraggled refugees from the torith raids. They remained wary and suspicious, but no one said or did anything.

Kaneth made a hissing sound and the two

Sansoths stepped back. "Tamith, I am well. Well enough," he said. He turned to look at Tom, then at the refugees. "And these are the human egg breakers."

"Now, wait," Tom said and stepped forward, despite a hissing from the Sansoth squad who grasped their weapons. "These people didn't know about your hatching ground. No one knew."

Perkins looked surprised. "Those eggs, uh—oh—they were the eggs of—of these people here?"

One of the women, mud in her hair, swallowed noisily.

"Yes. I'll explain later," Tom said. He turned to Kaneth. "How could they know?"

"We thought they were the eggs of those big dinosaur things," one of the refugees apologized.

Tamith made a throaty noise and his eyes slitted. His pale throat seemed to pulse and Tom stepped quickly between Perkins and the Sansoth warrior.

"Cool off," Tom said tautly. "It was an accident. Captain Kaneth, tell your men this was all a misunderstanding."

The big captain heaved himself erect and stood motionless as the medic sprayed his wounds with a foul-smelling liquid. The spray hardened, sealing the raw flesh. "Captain Swift," Kaneth said, "how would you feel if some alien creature massacred a hundred of your unborn offspring?"

"Ghastly," Tom admitted. "But when different races meet for the first time, they must expect surprises, even unfortunate accidents. I am certain that the Luna Corporation will make amends. We can't possibly restore your lost eggs, but we can help you to keep future eggs from being destroyed."

Kaneth glared at him. "How? Fight the torith?" He snorted loudly. "When the tor-ocka struck, what did you do? Nothing!"

"That's not true!" Ben said. "We couldn't fire for fear of hitting you!"

Kaneth's reptilian eyes bulged. "There is no honor in killing at a distance. You must be within reach of the fang and claw."

"There's not much honor in *any* kind of killing," Tom said. "Ben can tell you a lot about counting coup, of touching a live, armed enemy with a stick."

"With a *stick*?" Kaneth snapped.

"A test of bravery," Ben said. "Many of the tribes of my people did this. To come within touching distance, not to use a weapon, but merely to touch."

"Your people do not kill their enemies?" Tamith asked incredulously. Kaneth turned his massive head to look at his officer as Ben responded.

"I am afraid we did, at one time. Today—well, I guess we do it in court."

Kaneth stared at the boys, then said, "You will excuse my officer, Terrans. He hungers for a command, *any* command. Even my command." Kaneth exposed his big, sharp, yellow teeth. "As I said, we are a race who believes in the survival of the fittest, and Lieutenant Tamith believes he is the fittest."

Tamith said nothing, but a soft hiss briefly distorted his wide mouth.

Tom stepped in quickly. "I think we ought to be heading back. Captain Kaneth must have his wounds cared for, we must get these people some proper food, and—" He looked at Ben.

"And I can take a bath." The young Indian grinned.

Kaneth did not object as Tom led the small band of Terrans back toward camp. The Sansoth fell in behind and they trudged through the murky swamp until almost sunset.

Back at camp, they found Anita and Kate with seven more refugees, plus five others who had wandered in by themselves.

"I don't think there are any more," Perkins told Tom, after talking to the group.

"Terrible waste." Tom sighed. He glanced up from the map he had been studying. "We'll take one more party out into this area in the morning," he said, pointing. "If we find someone, great, but if not . . ." He shrugged sadly.

Ben got to his feet, edging past Mok N'Ghai and Aristotle to the opening in the tent that had been hastily erected. "I've got the next watch," he said. "Kate, you relieve me in four hours, right?"

The dark-haired young woman nodded, peering at the map.

"Well, listen," Perkins said. "I gotta say I'm relieved to get out of that swamp, and I thank you." He looked at each of them soberly, even at Aristotle. "I want you to know a lot of us think Luna sold us a bill of goods. Snowed us every inch of the way. Oh, he was good to us, but that's only because we were more efficient to him that way. We see it now."

"What are your plans?" Kate asked.

Perkins shrugged. "Well, to tell you the truth, I'm in no hurry to get back to Earth. I'd really like to go off exploring. See what's out there. Maybe—well, maybe we could find something that would be useful back home."

"Information is probably the most valuable

thing you can bring back," Tom said. He grinned and added, "There's something handy that just might work!"

"What?" Kate asked.

Tom stuck a thumb up. "The fortress. A movable city. Makes a great base while exploring a planet and a comfortable ship when you are traveling."

"But you—" Kate began.

"Oh, I can *unfix* the stardrive," Tom said. "Make it so it will work as often as you want, not just once, as it is now. What do you think?" he asked Perkins.

"I—boy—will they let us?"

"I think so. You're seasoned space explorers now. That's a rare breed." He smiled. "Kate, what about you? Did I detect something in your voice?"

Kate grinned a big, wide grin. "Tommy, my boy, you have just saved Auntie Kate from a terrible fate!" She stood up and her lithe body seemed to tense as she wrapped her arms around herself. Then her arms flew out and she let out a yell that startled everyone. In seconds, two Sansoth guards appeared at the tent flap, but Tom waved them away.

"I take it you like the idea?" the young inventor asked teasingly.

"I *love* it!" she said. Then she quickly sobered. "I can go, can't I? I mean, there's nothing to stop me?"

"It's a free universe," Tom said.

Kate One Star let out another yell, then dropped back into her chair. "Tommy, you don't *know* how I've wanted something like this! It's why I signed up with Luna in the first place. Earth has gotten so . . . so small, so tame!"

"Earth? Tame?" Anita asked, thinking of the great blizzards and the hurricanes, earthquakes, wars, volcanoes, droughts, and fires.

"Yes, tame!" Kate snapped. "There's nothing new there, nothing really dangerous. You know what can happen! No matter how bad it gets, it probably happened before. But not on some new world, not out there in the stars!"

Tom laughed. "Kate, I've never seen you so demonstrative!"

"I've never had reason before, Tom!" She turned to Perkins. "Listen, is it all right if I come along with you guys? I'm pretty good at my job."

"Ms. One Star, are you kidding? We'll probably elect you leader!"

Kate stared at him a moment. "You mean, uh, like captain?"

"Sure. Or whatever you want to call yourself. Boss Lady, Chief Honcho, whatever." Perkins looked very happy. "Let me go talk it over with Cazier, Bev Warren, Cliff, and the rest."

Kate stood up. "Don't you want to come, too?" she asked her friends. "You guys are pretty good, you know."

"Thanks, Kate," Tom said, "but we have to wind up all this." He gestured around him at the papers and equipment.

"Including finding the elusive David Luna," Mok N'Ghai said softly.

"Well, listen, you'll excuse me, huh?" Kate said. "I have some thinking to do. I've always been partial to the way the sky looks over in the space around Sirius," she added, leaving the tent.

There was a brief silence, then Tom asked Anita, "You want to go?"

Anita sat up. "Sure I want to. But I hope that the space fortress won't be the *only* ship going out to the stars. If you get my meaning."

"Noted," Tom said. "Now, if we—"

He broke off as shouts came from the darkness outside. There were cries and the sound of running feet. He leaped to the flap of the tent, stepping out as the others tumbled after him. "What's going on?" he shouted.

A Sansoth warrior came out of the darkness, a battle axe in his hand. Tom recognized Tamith.

"There's been an attack on the southern perimeter, Captain Swift!"

"Who attacked?" Tom demanded.

"Torith!" The reptilian warrior swung his axe toward the south. "They killed two of my warriors and one of yours."

Tom gasped at the news.

"That is not all, Captain. One of your men was carried off," Tamith added.

"Carried off? *Taken?* Who?" he asked, stepping closer to the Sansoth lieutenant.

"The one you call Ben!"

Chapter Fifteen

"*What!*" Tom cried. "Why would they take Ben?"

"I think I can answer that," Captain Kaneth said, striding out of the darkness. He carried a battle axe as well, but he slung it from his belt with slow deliberation.

"Your friend, or any living, breathing creature of sufficient size, is valuable to the torith. Undoubtedly, he will be a present to their queen."

"Queen?" Anita said. "I thought they were animals like, uh, dinosaurs."

"They are," Kaneth replied. "We do not know very much about them, but we know they have
156   their living spaces deep in the rock. And there

they have a queen. The one who gives birth to them all."

"Like the ant queen or the termite queen." Anita sighed.

"We had a warrior taken when we first landed here. We did not discover the entrance to their living space until too late. He had been shrouded with a membrane and was already dead." Kaneth made a gesture of resignation. "We left him there, to be food. That way the queen would not require another for a time."

With disgust in her voice, Anita said, "Why didn't you just kill this—this queen?"

"First of all, because we could not. There were too many of the toriths. And second, we would not. It would destroy the balance. Our eggs must be tested."

"You know something," Anita said, heat in her voice, "you guys are the—"

"Anita!" snapped Tom. "That will not help. Captain Kaneth, you think Ben was taken for food?"

The reptilian warrior nodded.

"And you know where this underground living area is?"

Again the Sansoth nodded.

"Will you take us there?"

The Sansoth slowly shook his head.

"But why not?" Angrily, Tom pointed into the darkness. "That's *Ben* out there, Captain! Benjamin Franklin Walking Eagle! My best friend. I'm not going to let him be carried off, be *eaten*—"

"The torith are not to be harmed, Terran," Kaneth said coldly. "You may attempt to find and rescue your friend. That is your privilege. But not at the cost of torith deaths."

"But the torith eat your eggs!" Anita protested.

"Precisely," the Sansoth officer responded. "It is part of the plan."

"Then we'll find the queen ourselves!" Tom snapped.

In a few moments, they were all assembled: Tom, Anita, Kate, Mok N'Ghai, and Aristotle.

"He's underground," Tom said, "but where?"

"We could use seismographic exploration," Anita said, "but all the instruments, the equipment—" She shrugged and gestured at the wasteland that had once been the base camp.

"I have that capability," Aristotle said. "If I had an explosion of some sort, preferably more than one, I could use the sound waves from the explosion to detect cavities in the ground. A hole of any size suitable for living space would show up."

"How will you do that?" Anita asked, curious.

"I can modify my speech sensor circuits to detect the waves. The explosion will be sound, just as speech is sound. It is a primitive method, but my radar is not sufficiently powerful to extend very far into the rock," Aristotle apologized.

"What sort of explosion would you need?" Kate asked.

"Nothing very large," the robot answered. "Two would be nice."

"Hmm," Kate mused. "I think I saw some EXP-12 in the security shed. The mud won't have hurt it. C'mon, Anita!" The two young women raced away, waving a hand light.

Tom looked at Mok N'Ghai and chewed at his lip. "Commander, the torith are not going to give Ben up easily. We may have to kill some of them."

"And you are wondering what the Sansoth might think?"

Tom nodded.

"If I read our reptilian friend correctly, he is treading a thin line," the Skree said. "He believes the torith are important to the testing of the youth, and he would like you to rescue your friend."

"Why do you think that?" Tom asked.

"Because he did not close the path completely. If you can find the entrance, and if you can find and rescue Ben, then it is what was intended; if not . . ." Mok N'Ghai made a grinding sound with his mandibles and waved his antennae.

"No help, but no hindrance, you mean?" Tom continued, chewing on his lip. "And he *did* tell us they were underground, in some burrow or hive or something. Then we'll—"

"Here!" Kate shouted as she and Anita came back. They both held red boxes of EXP-12. "Three, you can have three explosions!"

"Excellent," Aristotle said. "Can you arrange to have them go off at once?"

"A snap," Kate said, holding up some wire.

Within moments, Aristotle had suggested directions and distance. Tom, Anita, and Kate trotted off, lights bobbing, to plant the charges.

Minutes later, they were ready. Aristotle's hearing had been finely tuned and greatly enhanced. He had plunged a metal leg into the ground to act as a sounder. Now he took the detonator and ignited the charges himself, so he could measure to the microsecond.

Three flashes lit up the night and seconds later the explosions rolled over them. Birds squawked in the sky and grunting creatures splashed in the swamp.

"Well?" Tom asked impatiently.

"One kilometer south southwest is the largest cavity, but there is another, a smaller one, slightly

farther away from the first, to the south south-
east."

"Let's take the closest one first!" Tom said,
looking at a compass Kate gave him. "Mok
N'Ghai, will you accompany us to the cave
mouth? I want you to establish a defensive line.
When we come out, we may need protection."

"Of course, Tom."

"Aristotle, you'll—"

"May I accompany you? Ben is my friend, too,"
the mechanoid pleaded.

"It's a cave, old friend, and you are not the
most agile of warriors. And there is your inhibi-
tion against harming living creatures."

"Living *intelligent* creatures," the robot reminded him.

"Okay, come to the cave mouth. We'd probably
need your inertial guidance to save time, anyway."

"Thank you," the robot said.

To Anita, Tom said, "You stay here. Keep an
eye on the Sansoth. Use a radio to tell Aristotle if
anything happens." When Anita glared at him,
Tom grinned. "That's an order." The redheaded
young woman grimaced but nodded, watching
the searchers quickly fade to a cluster of bobbing
lights in the darkness of a hostile and alien
planet.

A short time later, their lights played on the

rocky cliff, bobbing in and out of the dark cave mouth to which Aristotle had unerringly led them. They hesitated. Were there guards? Traps? Alarms?

"Let's go," Tom said finally. His laser was in his hand, but he hoped he would not have to use it. "Take your positions!" Mok N'Ghai and the robot stationed themselves at opposite sides of the cave mouth.

"I believe this is an appropriate time to wish you good luck," Aristotle said.

Kate grinned at him in the dim beam from their weaving flashlights. "I thought you didn't believe in luck."

"Luck, good fortune—these are human names for chance," the robot answered. "Such sayings are linguistic shorthand to indicate good feeling on the part of the well-wisher."

"Trust Aristotle to clarify things," Kate sputtered as she followed Tom into the darkness.

The cave sloped downward and turned to the right. In a few moments Tom and Kate had lost sight of the dim patch of night sky behind them. Their flashlight beams ran over worn stone and reflected off small pools of water so clear they were almost invisible.

The young people splashed through the still pools until the tunnel climbed again. The strata of rock changed, then changed again as they started to descend once more. Patches of a quartzlike material appeared in the granite, reflecting their flashes back into their eyes.

"Oh!" Kate gasped as they turned a corner. Before them a beautiful crystalline wall, all pale lavender, orchid, and rose sparkled in their lights. "This is beautiful!" she whispered. The wall angled, then arched overhead until they found themselves in a narrow tunnel.

"Look at the ground," Tom said. "It's been roughly smoothed, the larger lumps chipped off, and shattered pieces wedged into the cracks."

"Who could have done that?" Kate wondered. "Are the torith intelligent after all?"

"Monkeys and gibbons are intelligent enough to do that," Tom replied. "They use a limited variety of tools. And these *are* alien creatures. Perhaps they just got tired of walking barefoot over sharp crystals."

Kate smiled happily at a huge outcropping of rose quartz. "I feel as if I'm in a gorgeous museum."

"Well," Tom whispered, "this one has strict rules."

"You mean we better not talk?"

Tom nodded. They walked carefully down along the sloping tunnel. Here and there appeared short drops, like giant steps, as tall as Tom.

After an hour, they emerged into a large cavern, four or five stories high. Blue crystal, shot with glimmering flecks of lavender and purple, twinkled all around them. The beauty of it made Kate exclaim in a soft voice, "I feel as if I were inside one of those beautiful Fabergé Easter eggs! It's lovely!"

Tom pointed at a patch of darkness on the opposite side and Kate nodded. The two young adventurers climbed up to the dark patch, which proved to be the opening of another tunnel. The blue crystals darkened quickly into purple as they crept along the passage. By the time they rounded a curve, the quartz crystals were blood red in color.

Suddenly, Tom put up a hand. A noise! Kate had heard it, too. Another noise. Turning off their lights, they moved quietly forward. They felt their way in the darkness with boot toes and fingertips, but after a few feet, Kate grabbed Tom's arm.

A pinkish light appeared ahead, reflecting off the red crystals. The noise became a kind of grunting chant, accompanied by an odd scuffling. Tom and Kate went closer to the light, then stopped, astonished by what they saw!

A cavern, larger than any they had seen, stretched in front of them, a great egg-shaped room hundreds of feet high. At the top glistened a wide patch of red crystals, casting a reddish light throughout the chamber. Tom realized the glowing patch must be very close to the surface. It was early morning now and the sunlight was coming through.

Standing on dozens of huge crimson crystal blocks were reptilian creatures unlike any he had seen before. They looked like skinny frogs, but were six feet tall. Their splayed feet stuck out to support their bowling-pin shape. Their wide mouths were open, and pink tongues flicked in and out from time to time. Their bulbous eyes seemed fixed on one spot and the two humans turned to look.

To their right was a massive block of white crystal, as big as a house. Standing in front of it were two figures. Human figures! Their arms were stretched out to either side and their wrists were held by the clawed hands of the froglike creatures.

Sacrifices! thought Tom. He blinked as he recognized just who the two "sacrifices" were: one was Ben, dark-haired and muscular, defiant and alert.

The other was David Luna!

Chapter Sixteen

All the figures were still. Even Ben and Luna were not moving. "What are they waiting for?" Kate whispered. Then Tom saw it.

From the overhead "skylight" of blood-red crystals came a single beam of white light. Somewhere in that mass was a maverick crystal, a clear one, as clear as glass. It passed down the rays of the sun, focusing them into a single white beam that wandered across the floor.

Tom watched it creep slowly up the side of a block of crimson quartz. In five minutes, it would touch the chunk of white crystal. Tom guessed that's when the sacrifices would begin. He could not suppress a shiver of terror.

The torith—and surely these were the egg-destroyers—were entirely silent. The preliminary chant was over, and only the faint sound of breathing was heard. Tom tried desperately to figure out what to do.

There were too many torith to fight and he had no reason to indiscriminately kill these creatures. Yet, his friend Ben was about to be sacrificed! The two torith standing near the human captives held a sharp shard of crystal in their taloned hands like ritual knives.

Tom thought furiously a moment, then put his mouth next to Kate's ear and whispered his plan to her. She grimaced, gave him a look of pain, then nodded. She unholstered her laser and lay low on the red floor.

Tom inhaled deeply as he, too, flattened himself on the sharp-edged crystals. He was taking the big chance of injuring someone, but he could think of nothing else that had even a slim chance of succeeding.

Their translating units would be useless in this, he knew, for it would all be over before the torith language was programmed in. Whatever was to be said would be gibberish to the giant frogs. It was going to have to be pure theater. And bluff. And nerve.

Tom gripped Kate's ankle and saw the combat

specialist nod. They tensed themselves, getting ready. Tom slapped her boot and stood up.

She rose, too, her laser flaring millipulses, spraying ruby-red beams at the opposite wall of the cavern and at the skylight overhead. The ruler-straight threads reflected off the smooth surfaces of the crystals, angling in different directions, striking other crystals, and reflecting again and again until the cabin was filled with a network of bright red beams.

Tom slipped over the tunnel edge into the cavern below, as all eyes went to the dramatic figure standing in the dimness of the cave mouth. Her right fist seemed to spout endless fire. Crystals cracked with the force of a gunshot, while others shattered as internal pressures were released.

Ping! Pock! Tüinnng! Crash!

The torith crouched, staring in shock at the human figure who kept up the barrage of fiery beams. One glanced off a crystal near Tom, crackling the surface and spraying out in weaker threads of red light.

The young inventor leaped from crystal block to crimson nugget, dodging around a stunned torith who did not see him. He reached the side of the white crystal and found some stepping stones, which he climbed two at a time. At that moment, the network of ruby beams crisscrossing the huge chamber stopped. For a moment, there was absolute silence.

Then Kate One Star began to speak.

"Into the valley of death rode the six hundred!" Kate thundered commandingly. "Cannons to the right of them! Cannons to the left of them!"

Tom slipped around the milky surface of the huge block and found himself a few feet from Ben. He saw his friend's eyes swing toward him and flutter a happy blink of recognition, but the young Indian did not move.

What now? thought Tom.

"William the Conquerer!" Kate exclaimed. "William Rufus, son of William the Conquerer! Henry the First! Stephen, nephew of Henry the First!"

Tom smiled faintly at the recitation of English rulers. He stepped forward and karate-chopped the torith holding Ben's right wrist. The creature staggered, blinked at him in slow motion, and fell down. The guard holding Ben's other wrist tugged at him, pulling the young man off balance. Then he raised his crystal knife and started toward Tom.

"Henry the Second!" declaimed Kate loudly, her voice echoing throughout the chamber.

"Richard the Second, Richard the Lion-Hearted!"

Ben tripped a third charging torith and Tom punched the knife-wielding guard in the stomach. The creature tumbled back, slipped off the crystal, and fell into a crack. Now the two torith holding David Luna started forward, but Luna struck at one of them.

"John Lackland, son of Henry the Second!" shouted Kate, waving her arms wildly.

Three humans versus three torith. A ritual knife slashed through Luna's shirt, scratching him, but a hard kick sent his opponent off the edge. In a moment, Tom and Ben had knocked down the other two froglike creatures and were running toward the steps, with Luna close behind.

"Henry the Third! Uh, Edward the First, Edward the Second, Edward the Third, Henry the Fourth, no, uh, Richard the Second!"

The dozens of torith stood as if mesmerized by the spectacle of the strange shouting. Tom, Ben, and Luna dodged and climbed until they were close to the tunnel mouth.

"Elizabeth the Second! Charles the Third!"

Tom stepped into the tunnel and Kate pointed her laser into the cavern, sending another score of millisecond pulses over the heads of the aliens.

The beams ricocheted off the crystal facets again and again as Tom led his group back up the tunnel.

Kate brought up the rear. "My . . . my laser's . . . finished," she puffed as they climbed.

Before Tom could answer, a roaring echoed in their ears. The torith had recovered from their stunned surprise and started to pursue the group.

"Give me your laser," Luna demanded of Tom. "I'll take care of those dirty—!"

"Keep moving," Tom snapped. He pushed Luna and Ben ahead, handing Ben the flashlight. He let Kate catch up, then motioned for her to go on ahead. "I'll be rear guard," he said. She nodded. His weapon was the only one with a charge left.

They ran as fast as they could. Luna tripped and fell, rolling in the crystal gravel, yelling with pain. Kate helped him to his feet and he snarled at her, snatching his arm from her grasp.

"Leave me alone!"

"Maybe we *should* have left you alone, Luna!" she snapped back.

"Move it, move it!" Tom urged, pushing them on. He looked back and thought he saw movement in the shifting shadows of the crystalline tunnel.

Tom fired several short bursts back down the tunnel, angling them at the walls where they bounced back and forth for a fraction of a second, creating a network of ruby-red light beams in the darkness. He heard harsh cries and scuffling sounds as he ran on.

The red crystals blended into purple, then lavender and blue. The young people and Luna climbed, descended, and were soon splashing their way through the still, invisible pools of pure cave water near the entrance.

"Aristotle!" Kate shouted. "It's us!"

They came up the incline toward the cave mouth wet and bruised. Mok N'Ghai met them and steadied them as the early morning light blinded them. "Quick!" he said. "We must get back to camp!"

"Get your insect hands off me, you ugly monster!" Luna snarled.

"Nothing like gratitude to warm your heart," Ben muttered.

"You didn't rescue me," Luna snapped at Tom. "You rescued your friend. I was just a bonus!"

"Keep moving," Tom cried. "They're right behind us."

The swampy jungle closed around them as they sprinted back toward the camp.

The Sansoth warriors were waiting for them

when they returned, along with the anxious human refugees. "What happened?" Cazier inquired.

"Were there deaths among the torith?" Kaneth asked in a hard voice.

"No," Tom said. "I don't think so. The laser loses a lot of strength when it's deflected. However—we're being chased by several dozen torith!"

The Sansoth commander blinked and stared past Tom. Then he turned to Tamith and grunted a command. "Double the perimeter guards! Order them to frighten off the torith!"

"Yes, sir," the officer answered, but when Kaneth moved away, Anita caught a strange look on the lieutenant's face. It was tricky trying to interpret alien expression, she knew, but she could have sworn Tamith felt a mixture of contempt and hatred.

"You have no jurisdiction over me!" David Luna said angrily to Tom. "This isn't even in the same part of the *galaxy* as Earth, much less Earth itself!"

"I'm making a citizen's arrest," Tom said calmly.

"I told you, you have no authority!" Luna snarled.

"Tom," Aristotle said, "I realize this is

precedent-setting and subject to future interpretation and analysis, but perhaps a standard code of Terran laws can be applied to human beings throughout space?"

Anita laughed. "I'll buy that. At least it's enough to trundle the great David Luna back home and see what they say."

"He'll probably buy his way out," Ben predicted gloomily.

"It would be needless!" Luna shrugged and leaned forward over the table in the center of the tent. "This is a new nation! Belle Genevieve belongs to *me*! I am ruler here! *You* are the trespassers!"

"They'll decide that back on Earth," Tom said. "When they—" He broke off as Captain Kaneth lumbered into the tent.

The Sansoth commander looked around at the group with ill-concealed hostility. A bug lit on his cheek and, in the wink of an eye, his tongue whipped at it, and it was gone—swallowed and gone.

"The torith are not attacking," he announced. "They circled twice, then disappeared, but they are still out there hiding, just waiting." He looked at Ben and Luna. "Did you harm the queen?"

"Queen?" Luna said, frowning. He was shocked when Tom quickly explained that he and Ben had been captured as food sacrifices to the torith queen.

"Ugh!" Luna shivered. "Disgusting creatures!" He gave both Kaneth and Mok N'Ghai venomous stares.

"Ben, see that Mister Luna is kept under guard," Tom said. "Deputize some of the workers."

Ben looked at Luna who was drawing himself up into a haughty figure, aloof and superior. "Think we can trust them? After all, it was Luna who hired them."

"And tricked them," Tom added. "Get Perkins to pick out some volunteers."

"Okay." Ben shrugged. "Come on, hotshot, it's the slammer for you."

"Take your ill-bred hands off me," Luna demanded.

Ben grinned. To Anita, Tom, and the others, he said, "You should have seen this guy trying to make a deal with the torith while we were waiting for the sun to come up. He offered them all of Belle Genevieve and half of New Jersey if they'd take me first. They didn't understand a word, of course."

"They're animals!" Luna said nastily.

"Right," Ben said. "But even animals have their ways. And the torith have theirs—meat sacrifices." He gestured at Luna from the tent flap. "Let's go, world conquerer."

As they left the tent, Kate entered and sat down. "Y'know," she said, "now I wish I had memorized *all* of 'The Charge of the Light Brigade' in school. That would have made a very impressive speech to the torith."

"You did just fine," Tom said smiling. "Great light show, too."

"I was afraid one of those beams would hit you. I had no control over how they bounced."

Tom shrugged, watching as Kaneth turned and left the tent without a word. "You know, we're going to have to keep a close eye on our slippery Mister Luna. He won't give up a rich prize like Belle Genevieve without a fight."

"He may do his fighting back in Terran courts." Kate yawned and stretched. "How about getting some sleep, huh? I'm exhausted. Let's retire to our nice little bunks on the *Exedra*."

Tom agreed and in a few moments only Aristotle was left standing silent and unmoving—but not unthinking.

It seemed like only seconds later that Ben shook Tom out of a sound sleep.

"Tom! Tom, wake up!" he cried.

"Wha—?" Tom rolled over.

"Luna's escaped!"

Chapter Seventeen

Tom's eyes popped open and he stared at Ben. "Luna *escaped*? How?"

"The Sansoth brought down another ship and—I don't know how—Luna got free and went aboard!" Ben explained.

"He can't work an alien spaceship all by himself!" Tom said, slipping into his jumpsuit. "Did any of the others go with him?"

"The Luna Corporation people? No, not as far as I can tell. But Tamith is gone. He went with Luna, and so did a number of Sansoth."

"Where's Kaneth?"

"In his ship. They are getting ready to go after them. He's calling his men in from the perimeter. That means no guards—"

"So the torith can attack!" Tom finished his friend's thought.

He leaped out of his cabin and raced down the passage to the airlock with Ben at his heels. Anita joined them, zipping up her green jumpsuit. Ben hastily filled her in as the airlock cycled. Then the trio raced across the swampy ground to the Sansoth ship. The reptilian warriors were filing in, kicking mud from their feet. Tom forced his way between them into the ship.

The first thing that hit him was the hot, muggy air. It was like a swamp, both in atmosphere and appearance. Amazed, he stopped to take in what he saw.

The passages were oval shaped and quite large, but all along the walls, set in and around the electronic and mechanical parts of the ship were metal boxes, each with a living plant in it. An intricate arrangement of water and drainage pipes serviced each container. The plants grew up and around the pipes. Blossoms hung near light fixtures and tendrils curled across the faces of dials and gauges.

The air was thick, warm, and filled with pollen and insects. The Sansoth warriors jostled Tom as they stomped in, and when he leaned toward a plant, the purple-leaved growth shrank back. Its violet flowers closed their petals, and thorns snapped out of pods along the stems.

Tom grabbed at a passing Sansoth. "Captain Kaneth— where is he?"

The warrior grunted, pointing forward. Followed by Ben and Anita, Tom ducked under some dark green leaves and made his way through the passage. Here and there were mounted polished metal plaques bearing an alien script.

The Terrans passed through a large room filling up with warriors strapping themselves into padded couches. A reluctant and suspicious officer let them into the control room.

Captain Kaneth turned in his chair to face them. Around him sat four Sansoth, bent over screens and banks of buttons. Even here were pots of plants, and the air was so hot and moist that Tom could hardly breathe.

"Captain, Luna has escaped—and kidnapped your ship!" Tom called out.

"No, Captain Swift, it was Tamith who stole our vessel. No doubt encouraged by your David Luna, but it is Tamith who stole."

"We must get Luna back!" Anita said. "He's a criminal!"

"So is Tamith," Kaneth rumbled. "And we

shall find and punish him!" He stared at the humans. "Get off my ship now. I am going to leave, and I do not want you aboard." His head snapped to the left and he said, "Gorim! Signal for lift in one minute!"

"Wait, Captain," Tom said. "Why would Lieutenant Tamith go off with Luna? Was he not a loyal officer?"

"Tamith—now dead to his clan and his name to be struck from the rolls—was ambitious. He thought himself a better leader than I." Kaneth's talon gestured. "He attempts to prove it. But he is dead."

"You guys are sure tough on each other," Ben said.

Kaneth eyed him gloomily. "We are survivors, human. We will outlive all the races of the universe. I pursue Tamith. If he wins, he is the strongest and the clan continues. You have thirty seconds to leave."

"Come on," Tom said. "No use talking to him." They ran back through the ship, slipped past an impatient guard at the airlock, and ran out into the camp.

The Sansoth vessel lifted with a roar and Tom began shouting at the human refugees. "Get aboard the *Exedra*! We'll take off in five minutes!"

Tom found Aristotle and Mok N'Ghai already

in the control room, giving the spaceship the preflight check. He reached over and flicked a switch. "Perkins? Cazier? Is everyone aboard?"

"Everyone," Perkins said.

"You're sure? No one left behind?"

"Are you kidding?" Perkins exclaimed. "No one is going to stay on this planet!"

As Tom settled into the pilot's couch, he saw movement at the edge of the swamp. The torith were moving in! "Are we ready to lift?" Tom asked Mok N'Ghai.

"Yes," the Skree replied. "Take her up, Captain."

The *Exedra* moved away from the planet smoothly. The stench and mugginess of Belle Genevieve seemed to drain away. In a few seconds, the sky darkened and they were in space.

"Where are Luna and Tamith, Aristotle?" Tom asked.

"Third quadrant, twenty-eight south, sixteen north. And Tom, I've linked into the Sansoth computer. They are making calculations for a hyperspace jump!"

"We'll never catch them!" Anita cried. Kate crowded into the control room, taking in the situation on the screens in one practiced look.

"The danger is great," Aristotle warned.

"What's he mean?" Kate asked Tom.

"When a ship goes into hyperspace, there is a great deal of warpage in the immediate area. That's why we go out away from the planets and moons before we do it," Tom said, punching up a program on a nearby screen. "If two ships are close enough . . ." He hesitated. "You know, all this is pretty new. Mok N'Ghai?"

"It is as you suspected, Tom. The magnetic and gravitational forces on each ship would be immense. The worst that could happen is one or both would be torn apart. Literally. The *least* that could happen is that each is pulled from its intended course."

"Uh-oh," Kate said. On a screen, a readout showed the positions, trajectories, and possible future intersection of the two Sansoth ships. "Doesn't Kaneth *know?*" she asked.

Mok N'Ghai made a gritting sound with his mandibles and briefly his antennae dipped. "He knows. But the Sansoth are a proud and, um, noble race who claim to know no fear."

"Proud and stupid, it sounds to me," Kate said.

"It is a matter of honor to Captain Kaneth," the Skree explained.

"I'm not knocking honor," Kate replied, "but this is playing with fire. Luna could pop into hyperspace at any moment."

"Not for some thirteen minutes, forty seconds," Aristotle said. "But at any time after that, yes."

Tom flicked a switch. "Put me on Luna's frequency," he said to the robot.

The robot pressed two buttons. "Proceed," he said.

"Luna, this is the *Exedra*. Over," Tom called. He waited, then repeated the sentence. In the midst of Tom's third try, Luna came on the air.

"*Exedra*, this is David Luna. I shouldn't even bother with a loser like you, Swift, but I just can't help gloating. It is a basic character flaw, I know. But it is *so* satisfying."

"Luna, don't you know what will happen if either you or your pursuer go into hyperspace? You'll be torn apart!"

Luna chuckled. "Swift, you don't scare me! Yes, the pressures could rip us apart, but they are more likely to just throw us off."

"You'll—"

"I know you mean well, all your kind do. But you don't understand the situation. So what if we are thrown off our intended course? What difference does it make? We are not going to any specific star! Just away, away from your stifling laws, away from the petty people—!"

"With a shipload of Sansoth?" the young inventor interrupted.

"I don't need people, Swift. I would prefer humans, but that is mere planetary chauvinism. You'll discover that I have one of your clever little translation units. I'll have it duplicated so I can go anywhere, talk to anyone. I'll create a whole new empire." David Luna paused dramatically before adding, "*Then* I'll come back to Earth!"

"I thought you didn't need anyone!" Kate snapped, leaning toward the microphone.

"But I do have my ego, my dear. I told you I was flawed. It will suit me just fine to return a conquerer, to make the governments of Earth deal with me as an equal." Luna laughed. "Equal to all of Earth, of course!"

"And Tamith?" Tom said. "He's your servant?"

"Nicely done. Driving a wedge between me and my faithful assistant. But the translator's turned off. The reptile cannot understand what we are saying. He thinks we are partners."

Luna laughed again. "I must say I was brilliant. I could sell a used car to a fish. I painted a beautiful picture of what he and I could do together. My brains and his brawn, you know. Very ambitious, my Tamith, a true son of the noble Sansoth."

Tom did not comment, and Luna went on, "Well, there's a winner and loser in every contest,

Mister Swift, and we know which we are. We'll be going into hyperspace soon."

"Tom," Aristotle said, "if we do not want to get caught, we had better veer off. We will be in normal space as they go into hyperspace. The tensions could easily tear us—"

"Veer off!" Tom ordered. Mok N'Ghai's delicate fingers punched a series of commands and the *Exedra* swung away.

"Ah, very sensible, Swift," Luna said over the radio. "Not so sensible is our Captain Kaneth. I really don't know what he expects to do. Grapple and board us like some ancient pirate who—No, Tamith! What are you doing? It doesn't matter—Tamith! Don't shoot! We will leave him behind with the other losers!"

Tom looked at his friends. "Tamith wants to fight," he said. "It sounds like Luna is having problems with his 'partner.'"

"Kaneth's pursuit is a challenge," Mok N'Ghai explained.

"You fool!" Luna roared. "Look, in seconds we can be—" There was a crashing sound and some noises Tom could not identify. Then Luna's voice came again. "You stupid iguana! No, I won't permit it! It's idiotic to stop and fight them, we—!" Luna screamed in anger and pain and there were more shouts.

"I'll—you ignorant *lizard*! I'm going to—"

Then there was silence.

The next moment, the two dots blinked out on the *Exedra*'s screen!

Chapter Eighteen

"Where . . . where did they go?" Anita gasped.

"Somewhere very far away," Ben said grimly.

"How terrible!" Kate shuddered.

"Oh, they may not be hurt," Tom said. "What do you think, Mok N'Ghai?"

"They were close enough to affect each other, yet . . . not too close. But Captain Kaneth's ship was still operating in normal space. It was either taken into hyperspace, too, or . . ." The insectoid commander shrugged.

"We're all right?" Kate asked.

Tom scanned the dials and screens and nodded. "Back to the fortress," he ordered.

"Okay." Kate stepped to the control room hatch.

"I'll go alert the others," Ben said, following Kate.

Anita moved closer to Tom, who stood behind the Skree and the robot. "You think Luna's alive?" she asked, looking at the screen that had tracked the two Sansoth ships.

Tom shrugged. "It's certainly possible, but I don't think we'll be seeing him for a while."

Anita chuckled. "Things were certainly lively when he was around!"

Tom made a face. "Luna was a greedy, ambitious egomaniac, the kind of person who thinks of others as pawns or toys. He used charm as a tool, not as a manifestation of his personality."

"Oh, I know all that. But he was a human being." Anita gestured around her. "And humans are not all that common out here." She smiled.

"They will be," Mok N'Ghai predicted.

The young people laughed. "What makes you say that?" Tom asked.

"I have observed you for some time now, under various kinds of stress," the Skree said. "You are tough. You are not perfect, but you adapt quickly. Perhaps you are not truly representative of your race—I am not of mine. One must be brave, intelligent, and resourceful to go into space. It takes a certain kind. The curious, the restless, even the unhappy and the fearful."

"Fearful?" Anita asked.

"People do many things out of fear. Fear that if they stay home, it will be worse. Fear of being left behind. It does not matter. You humans will spread out now. You are crude, true, but you accept a challenge."

One of Mok N'Ghai's spindly, insectoid arms made a gesture at the stars. "That is the greatest challenge of all. Any race that does not accept it—that does not try—will die. Not physically, perhaps, but morally. Others that do accept the challenge will grow."

"Why, Mok, that was some speech!" Anita said, clapping her hands.

"A true one," Tom added.

"I will be most appreciative if I am allowed to assist in future exploration," Aristotle spoke up.

"We won't leave home without you," Tom promised him with a smile. "But first, some unfinished business!"

Kate One Star stood in the airlock of the *Exedra,* smiling at her friends. "Listen, I want you to know, it's—well, it's been really great with you. But there's a candy store out there in space, and I just can't resist it." There was the hint of wetness in her eyes and, even more than that, in the eyes of Tom, Ben, and Anita. Mok N'Ghai made a soft clicking sound. Only Aristotle stood completely still.

"Go get 'em, *Captain,*" Ben told his cousin.

"Captain," Kate mused. "Can you imagine that? *Me?*"

"None better!" Anita declared.

"Well, it's time," Kate said. She took a deep breath, then, in quick succession, hugged Anita, kissed Ben on the cheek, startled Mok N'Ghai with a sharp clicking noise, patted Aristotle, and kissed Tom. Then, in a graceful, sudden movement, she ducked out the airlock hatch.

Tom sat down in the control chair and switched off the magnetic locks. The *Exedra* drifted away from the space fortress, now called the *Star of Magellan* to purge it of any Luna Corporation connotation.

The planetary drive fired up on the *Magellan* and the two ships separated at an accelerated pace. Anita turned to Mok N'Ghai. "What was the meaning of that sound Kate made? It seemed to surprise you."

"Um, yes. It was an expression of love used by our people. Race to race, person to person."

Anita's gaze went to the port where the quickly

dwindling *Magellan* could be seen. "We love you, too, Katie," she whispered.

Soon the ship became only a blip on a screen. Tom punched out navigational directions and the *Exedra* swung about to head for Earth.

"Homeward bound." Ben sighed. Little did he know that they would only spend a short time there because a new space adventure awaited them in *Ark Two*.

"Earth will always be home," Tom said, "but—"

All eyes went to the screen showing the stars in every direction around them.

The universe glittered and shone in a hundred colors. Nebulae were flung like veils across fields of fiery suns. Galaxies burned by the million, stars by the hundreds of million.

This, too, was home!

THE TOM SWIFT® SERIES
by Victor Appleton

The City in the Stars (#1)
Terror on the Moons of Jupiter (#2)
The Alien Probe (#3)
The War in Outer Space (#4)
The Astral Fortress (#5)
The Rescue Mission (#6)

You will also enjoy

THE HARDY BOYS® SERIES
by Franklin W. Dixon

Night of the Werewolf (#59)
Mystery of the Samurai Sword (#60)
The Pentagon Spy (#61)
The Apeman's Secret (#62)
The Mummy Case (#63)
Mystery of Smugglers Cove (#64)
The Stone Idol (#65)
The Vanishing Thieves (#66)
The Outlaw's Silver (#67)
The Submarine Caper (#68)
The Four-Headed Dragon (#69)
The Infinity Clue (#70)